Homer, Alexander Pope

Pope - The Iliad of Homer

Books I. VI. XXII. XXIV - Volume 1

Homer, Alexander Pope

Pope - The Iliad of Homer
Books I. VI. XXII. XXIV - Volume 1

ISBN/EAN: 9783337090302

Printed in Europe, USA, Canada, Australia, Japan

Cover: Foto ©Andreas Hilbeck / pixelio.de

More available books at **www.hansebooks.com**

POPE

THE ILIAD OF HOMER

BOOKS I. VI. XXII. XXIV.

EDITED

WITH NOTES AND AN INTRODUCTION

BY

ALBERT H. SMYTH

PROFESSOR OF THE ENGLISH LANGUAGE AND LITERATURE
IN THE CENTRAL HIGH SCHOOL OF PHILADELPHIA
MEMBER OF THE AMERICAN PHILOSOPHICAL SOCIETY

New York

THE MACMILLAN COMPANY

LONDON: MACMILLAN & CO., Ltd.

1899

All rights reserved

Norwood Press
...shing & Co. — Berwick & Smith
Norwood Mass. U.S.A.

CONTENTS

INTRODUCTION

GOLDWIN SMITH has called the translation of Homer into verse "the Polar Expedition of literature, always failing, yet still desperately renewed." The comparison is just. It is indeed a famous and difficult voyage, undertaken by many brave and spirited adventurers, but with complete success by none. The most accomplished scholars and poets have attempted to convey to the English reader the resounding lines of Homer, and the grace, vigor, and dignity of Homeric life. Chapman, Hobbes, Pope, Cowper, Derby, Merivale, Newman, Worsley, and Bryant have exhausted their scholarship and skill in the task. But Homer still defies modern reproduction. "His primeval simplicity is a dew of the dawn which can never be distilled."

Matthew Arnold's acute and suggestive essay "On Translating Homer" contains much practical advice, both in negative and positive counsels. Mr. Arnold believed that the translator should be penetrated by

a sense of four qualities of his author — "that he is
eminently rapid; that he is eminently plain and
direct, both in the evolution of his thought and in
the expression of it, that is, both in his syntax and
in his words; that he is eminently plain and direct
in the substance of his thought, that is, in his matter
and ideas; and, finally, that he is eminently noble."
For want of duly penetrating themselves with these
qualities of Homer the translators have failed to
render him; Cowper fails in speed, Pope in plainness
and directness of style, Chapman in plainness and
directness of ideas, and Newman in "nobleness."

According to Mr. W. J. Courthope all English
translations of Homer may be said to be comprised
in three classes. The first is represented by Chapman
and is the method followed by Pope's predecessors;
its object is to reproduce the *sense* of the original.
The second is represented by Cowper and is the
method followed by every subsequent translator; its
aim is "not only to reproduce Homer's sense as
literally as possible, but also to reproduce his style
in an epic manner peculiar to the English language."
The third is the method of Pope. "Pope's purpose,"
says Mr. Courthope, "is to master the general sense of
what he is about to render, and then to give this in
such rhetorical forms as his own style requires, omit-
ting and even adding thoughts at his pleasure."

In every great poem there is a residuum which cannot be transferred from one language to another. In the case of Homer the vehicle of translation and the very manner of modern thinking and feeling are alien to the Homeric character. Chapman is faithful to his original, but his loose, archaic, fanciful style and long ballad-metre are out of keeping with the epic elevation of the *Iliad*. Cowper adopted the Miltonic blank verse as an English equivalent for the Greek hexameters, and believed that in his translation he was adhering closely to his original, — "the matter found in me," he said, "whether the reader like it or not, is found also in Homer; and the matter not found in me, how much soever the reader may admire it, is found only in Mr. Pope." But Cowper failed, as Mr. Arnold said, to render the bright equable speed of Homer, and his translation is dull and monotonous.

Pope was notoriously no Grecian. He wrote to Parnell, who made him a present of the "Essay on Homer" which is prefixed to his translation, "You are a generous author, I a hackney scribbler; you are a Grecian, and bred at a University, I a poor Englishman of my own educating." But whatever his inaccuracies, Pope succeeded in fascinating the world with his "clarion couplets." He entered into the action of the poem and told the story with grace and animation. "A pretty poem, Mr. Pope, but it is not Homer," said the famous Greek scholar Richard Bentley. Nevertheless Pope had so caught the spirit of adventure, he sympathized so genuinely with the bravery of the heroes and entered with such delight into their exhortations and invectives, that his translation leaped at once into popularity and has ever since commanded the praise that belongs to a great original poem.

The sonnet is famous in which Keats, who knew no Greek though he was deeply imbued with the spirit of the Greeks, describes his rapture on first looking into Chapman's Homer : —

> "Then felt I like some watcher of the skies
>   When a new planet swims into his ken,
> Or like stout Cortes when with eagle eyes
>   He stared at the Pacific — and all his men
> Looked at each other with a wild surmise —
>   Silent — upon a peak in Darien."

Many more readers, the younger ones particularly, remember the rapture of their first introduction to Homer in the ringing lines of Pope. Emerson used to say he would as soon think of swimming the Charles River every time he went to Boston as of reading all his books in their original tongue. Pope's translation is a great English classic, and it embalms forever the supreme ideality of Homer which veins all

modern literature. Professor Jebb has a fine phrase
for those precious things of art, whether literature, or
sculpture, or architecture, that have been recovered
from the ancient civilization. He calls them "salvage
from centuries of ruin." The Homeric poems saved
and transmitted across the centuries have been the
foundation of human culture and "the very fountain-
head of all pure poetic enjoyment, of all that is spon-
taneous, simple, native, and dignified in life."

Frederic Harrison in his impatience at the neglect
of Homer and the eternal works of genius wrote in
his admirable little volume on *The Choice of Books*,
"One knows — at least every schoolboy has known —
that a passage of Homer, rolling along in the hexam-
eter or trumpeted out by Pope, will give one a hot
glow of pleasure and raise a finer throb in the pulse;
one knows that Homer is the easiest, most artless, •
most diverting of all poets; that the fiftieth reading
rouses the spirit even more than the first — and yet
we find ourselves (we are all alike) painfully pshaw-
ing over some new and uncut barley-sugar in rhyme,
which a man in the street asked us if we had read, or
it may be some learned lucubration about the site
of Troy by some one we chanced to meet at dinner.
It is an unwritten chapter in the history of the human
mind, how this literary prurience after new print un-
mans us for the enjoyment of the old songs chanted

forth in the sunrise of human imagination. To ask a
man or woman who spends half a lifetime in sucking
magazines and new poems to read a book of Homer
would be like asking a butcher's boy to whistle
'Adelaida.' The noises and sights and talk, the whirl
and volatility of life around us, are too strong for us.
A society which is forever gossiping in a sort of perpetual 'drum' loses the very faculty of caring for
anything but 'early copies' and the last tale out.
Thus like the tares in the noble parable of the sower,
a perpetual chatter about books chokes the seed which
is sown in the greatest books of the world." (Harrison, *Choice of Books*, p. 29.)

ALEXANDER POPE

An interesting allegorical picture painted by Hogarth
for the Elephant, a public house in Fenchurch Street,
London, is now preserved in Sudeley Castle. It represents the blindfolded goddess of fortune standing
on a globe elevated above the earth, and holding in
each hand an inverted bag, from which favors and
evils are descending. Beneath is the fast-flowing
stream of life, and upon the bridge stands the artist,
while Richardson, the novelist, hands him a bag of
gold. Advancing toward the place where the benig-
nant showers of fortune are descending, Alexander

Pope appears in a car drawn by a swan with seven necks, emblematical of the *trivium* and *quadrivium* — the seven liberal arts and sciences. Following the car is a motley crew of critics, with faces distorted with passion, armed with sticks and spears, typical of the lances of calumny, with which they are about to assail the poet. Familiar faces are visible in the crowd; Dennis, Theobald, Curl, and Mist are there, and Cibber the laureate, and Henley the orator.

The poet who is thus between kind fortune and evil tongues is the translator of the *Iliad*, and the author of the *Dunciad*. By his translation he acquired a European reputation, a position of ease and independence, and that familiarity with the leading representatives of the English aristocracy which was one of the chief goals of his ambition.

But his way of life was beset with quarrels. He was thoroughly versed in the art of making enemies, and seemed at times, so waspish was his tongue, so vitriolic his humor, to be "instinct with life malignant." His vanity, his untruthfulness, his irritability, and his arrogance may, with reason and with charity, be explained as proceeding from his physical infirmities. His life, he said, was "one long disease." He was short of stature — a high chair necessary to bring him to the level of an ordinary dining-table; his legs were thin and wrapped in many folds of linen, his body so crooked that he was nicknamed an interrogation point, and he was tormented with constant headaches. Few writers are more familiar to us through caricature and description. The dress and the habits of Dr. Johnson are not better known than Pope's paddings and stays, his wadded canvas jackets, and his twice doubled hose. His countenance drawn and pinched, his delicate features, his large blue expressive eyes, we know from Roubiliac's and Rysbrach's busts of him, and the portraits by Kneller, Jervas, Hoare, and Richardson.

Pope was born in the city of London of an obscure Roman Catholic family, in the year of the glorious Revolution of 1688 (May 21). His father conducted the wholesale business of a linen merchant in Lombard Street, a street which to the English ear, as De Quincey says, possessed a degree of historical importance: "first, as the residence of those Lombards, or Milanese, who affiliated our infant commerce to the matron splendors of the Adriatic and the Mediterranean; next, as the central resort of those jewellers, or goldsmiths, as they were styled, who performed all the functions of modern bankers from the period of the Parliamentary War to the rise of the Bank of England."

In 1700 the successful tradesman retired from business, to Binfield, in Windsor Forest, where the family lived upon an estate of twenty acres, and where a part

of the house and an ancient row of Scottish firs still
remain as in Pope's childhood. Very little is recorded
of his early years. When eight years old he began to
study Latin and Greek under the direction of a priest;
for a short time he studied at a Roman Catholic school
at Twyford, near Winchester, and afterwards under
Thomas Deane at Marylebone.

While his education was desultory and superficial,
he read widely and constantly, "like a boy gathering
flowers"; indeed it was said that he did nothing else
but write and read. His first acquaintance with
Homer came in his twelfth year, through Ogilby's
translation; he wrote an epic of Alexander between
his thirteenth and fifteenth years; and while still a
child came up to London from Windsor Forest and
gazed with reverence and enthusiasm upon the face of
old John Dryden upon what must have been one of
his last appearances at Will's Coffee-house.

Among Pope's early acquaintances and patrons were
Sir William Trumbull, with whom he rode out every
day; William Walsh, who recommended Pope to make
correctness his study and aim; and Wycherly, forty-
eight years his senior, from whom he learned much of
fashion and of wit. The Catholic boy, without name
or rank or fortune, was honored and caressed because
of his single-hearted devotion to literature.

Sir William Trumbull encouraged him to write the

"Pastorals," which Jacob Tonson, the publisher, issued in 1709 in a volume of "Miscellany," which began with the pastorals of Ambrose Philips and ended with those of Pope. According to his own account Pope was but sixteen years old when these poems were written, but all his assertions with regard to himself are to be received with caution, as it is well known "that he systematically antedated his compositions in order to obtain credit for precocity." With his introduction to literary and aristocratic society Pope affected the tone of Will's Coffee-house. The chief literary influences of the time proceeded from the coffee-houses; the politicians met at the St. James's, the critics at Will's, and the scholars at the Grecian. The clubs, a little later, took the place of the coffee-houses; and with the development of party spirit arose a demand for facile and fertile literary brains to aid the party leaders. Addison, who had been one of the society at Will's, gathered about him a party of Whig pamphleteers and poets who held their meetings at Button's, and who were called "the little senate." Pope became acquainted with Addison and his circle, and with Swift, after the publication of the "Essay upon Criticism" (1711), in which he presented in verse his reflections upon the principles of his art. Addison praised the work in the *Spectator*, December 20, 1711, but regretted "some strokes of personality" in the

poem. Pope immediately wrote to Steele acknow-
ledging the praise and promising to amend the objec-
tionable matter, and Steele in turn introduced Pope
to Addison. His next poem, "Windsor Forest," mod-
elled upon "Cooper's Hill," appeared in 1713. It was
animated by a Tory spirit, anticipated the Peace of
Utrecht, and brought Pope the friendship of Swift.
He soon became a member of the Scriblerus Club, and
was upon intimate terms with Gay, Parnell, Arbuthnot,
Congreve, Atterbury, and Oxford.

The "Rape of the Lock" — "the most exquisite
monument of playful fancy that universal literature
offers" — was published in 1714, though part of it
had appeared two years before. The "amorous cause"
of the "dire offence" depicted in the poem was an
incident that concerned two prominent members of
Roman Catholic society. Lord Petre, a young man
of twenty, had clipped a lock of hair from the head
of Arabella Fermor, a celebrated beauty of the day,
and John Caryll — a person of some authority with
the Roman Catholic party — suggested to Pope to
celebrate the petty quarrel in a poem, and so to recon-
cile the pair. The mock-heroic poem instantly won
popular favor, and three thousand copies of it were
sold in four days. It was Sir William Trumbull who
first suggested to Pope the translation of the *Iliad*,
April 9, 1708. But Pope knew no Greek and had

scarcely the courage for the task. In the autumn of 1713, however, he announced his intention of translating Homer. Lord Lansdowne and Joseph Addison expressed their gratification, and wrote to him encouragingly. In November (1713) Bishop Kennet, describing in his diary an occasion when Dean Swift led the conversation, says: "Then he instructed a young nobleman that the best poet in England was Mr. Pope (a Papist), who had begun a translation of Homer into English verse, for which he must have them all subscribe; for, says he, the author shall not begin to print till I have a thousand guineas for him."

A thousand guineas was a great sum for any literary enterprise to yield, but as the sequel proved Swift underestimated the extraordinary success of this particular undertaking. The work was designed on a magnificent scale; it was to be printed in six sumptuous volumes at a guinea a volume. Pope was to have all the subscriptions, and a copyright from the publisher, Bernard Lintot, of £200 for each volume. The number of subscribers to the *Iliad* was 574, and the number of copies subscribed for was 654. Consequently by the subscription Pope obtained six times 654 guineas, or slightly more than £4000, which, with the copyright (£1200 for the work) swelled Pope's profits upon the transaction to £5300. The translation of the *Odyssey*, likewise published by subscription, was only a trifle less remunerative. The colossal labors of the venture were lightened by a partnership in toil; Pope "let off," as De Quincey says, to sub-contractors several portions of the undertaking, like modern contractors for a loan. Broome and Fenton, the collaborators, between them translated twelve books, and Pope undertook the other twelve. Fenton received £300, and Broome £500. By the subscription to the *Odyssey* Pope received £3000 (574 copies subscribed for at a guinea for each of the five quarto volumes), and for the copyright £600 additional from Lintot, the publisher.

"The jingling of the guinea" has a significance in this instance which renders the commercial aspect of the publication peculiarly interesting.

In the first place, it was "unquestionably the greatest literary labor, as to profit, ever executed, not excepting the most lucrative of Sir Walter Scott's, if due allowance be made for the altered value of money" (De Quincey). And in the second place, it secured ease and independence to Pope for the rest of his life. He bought an annuity of some £500, and a long lease of an estate of five acres upon the Thames, at Twickenham, where he lived until his death, cultivating his gardens and lampooning his adversaries.

Pope was at first oppressed with the magnitude of his task. He said to Spence: "In the beginning of my translating the *Iliad* I wished anybody would hang me a hundred times. It sat so heavily on my mind at first that I often used to dream of it, and do sometimes still."

To Jervas, he wrote, when in full career, July 28, 1714: "What can you expect from a man who has not talked these five days? Who is withdrawing his thoughts as far as he can, from all the present world, its customs and its manners, to be fully possessed and absorbed in the past. When people talk of going to church, I think of sacrifices and libations; when I see the parson, I address him as Chryses, priest of Apollo; and instead of the Lord's Prayer, I begin: —

'God of the silver bow,' etc.

While you in the world are concerned about the Protestant succession, I consider only how Menelaus may recover Helen, and the Trojan war be put to a speedy conclusion."

Pope was not a scholar; his knowledge of languages, ancient and modern, was maimed and imperfect. Voltaire said he could hardly *read* French, and spoke not one syllable of the language. De Quincey avowed his belief in Pope's thorough ignorance of Greek when he commenced his translation. He mastered the sense of the original from the English versions of his predecessors, Chapman, Hobbes, and Ogilby, and from the

French translations of La Vallérie and Dacier, and the Latin version of Eobanus Hessius. When it became necessary to consult the commentators and critics who, said Pope, "lie entrenched in the ditches, and are secure only in the dirt they have heaped about them with great pains in the collecting it," he called upon Parnell for assistance who wrote for the translation an "essay upon Homer." The notes of Eustathius, the Archbishop of Thessalonica, were translated for him by Broome, and Jortin, a young Cambridge scholar.

The social success of the work was also remarkable. Pope was invited to the country houses of Lord Harcourt, Lord Bathurst, and Lord Digby, and in April, 1716, he moved to Chiswick "under the wing of my Lord Burlington" in order to be near the aristocratic society of the Thames. John Gay's poem "Mr. Pope's Welcome from Greece" names pleasantly the distinguished people who congratulated Pope upon the completion of his translation. He entertained at Twickenham in his thrifty way, "watching his butler very sharply, and by reason of his infirmities, was very measured in his wine-drinking. Swift, who used to come and pass days with him, may have made the glasses jingle: and there were other worthy friends who, when they came for a dinner, kept the poet in a tremor of unrest. The Prince of Wales, after the

Georges of Hanover had come in, used sometimes to honor the poet with a visit; and the rich and powerful Bolingbroke — what time he lived at Battersea — used to come up in his barge, landing at the garden entrance — as most great visitors did — and discuss with him those faiths, dogmas, truisms, and splendid generalities which afterward took form in the famous *Essay on Man.*" [1]

The rest of Pope's life is little else than a record of "disease, publication, and quarrels." His satirical powers found their fullest exercise in the *Dunciad* (1728–9), in which he bestowed all his venom upon his libellers, reviewers, and rivals. The professed action of the poem is "the restoration of the reign of Chaos and Night by the ministry of Dulness, in the removal of her imperial seat from the City to the Polite World." The Hero of the Poem — the arch-ruler of this realm of *Dulness* — is Theobald, — "poor, piddling Tibbald," — to whose poverty and dulness an entire book of the *Dunciad* is devoted, and who is exalted to this bad eminence solely because he had ventured in his *Shakespeare Restored* to point out

---

[1] Quoted from D. G. Mitchell, *English Lands, Letters, and Kings*, Vol. III., 1895. A work of rare attractiveness, in which the great figures of literature are made to live again by virtue of the author's acute sympathy, intimate knowledge, and faultless English.

the blunders that Pope had perpetrated in his *Edition of Shakespeare* (1725). This publication marks the culmination of his career; to use De Quincey's comparison: "like a hornet, who is said to leave his sting in the wound, and afterwards to languish away, Pope felt so greatly exhausted by the efforts connected with the *Dunciad* that he prepared his friends to expect for the future only an indolent companion and a hermit." Time, too, was dissolving the circle of his friends. Atterbury, the attainted and banished Bishop, died in 1732; Gay died suddenly at the close of the same year, and the fatal blight of madness was possessing Dean Swift, who from the beginning of their acquaintance maintained unbroken a strange affectionate friendship for the sensitive crippled poet. His mother, whom he had tenderly loved and watched over, and who in her senile dotage recognized no face but that of her son, died in 1733 at a great age, at Twickenham. His writings now were half-moral, half-satirical; and his philosophy and poetry in *The Epistle to Lord Burlington, Essay on Man, Epistle to Arbuthnot,* etc., were blended in a style whose burnished lustre is unequalled in literature.

His last effort was the fourth book of the *Dunciad* (1742), the conclusion of which is one of the greatest accomplishments of his life. The "long disease" was now drawing to an end; he became weak and, at

times, delirious; Lord Bolingbroke and a few stanch
friends sustained him.   He died May 30, 1744.

POPE'S VERSIFICATION

The rhymed couplet — commonly called the *classical
couplet* — was the prevalent poetic measure of the age
of Dryden and the age of Pope.   That measure is
generally recognized as a reform of the license and ex-
travagance that marked the unregulated flow of verse
in the late Elizabethan days.   It belonged as naturally to the classical or "correct" manner in poetry,
as did the preceding metres to the romantic manner.   The varied stanza metres of the Elizabethans
declined at length into the disorderly blank verse of
the dramatists.   The literary style retained its vehe-
mence when the emotions that had created it had
subsided.   The genuine utterance of Marlowe and
Shakespeare became the inane rant of such writers as
Cyril Tourneur.   Desperately striving to maintain
the traditions of the great age, the post-Elizabethan
poets strained their plots and their language to supply
the place of failing originality.   They stimulated,
with impossible horrors and violent diction, the jaded
public taste until stimulants ceased to compel even
a momentary spasm of attention.   The change that
then took place by which poetry lost its violence, and

a new and different order began in the technic of
verse, has been defined as the formal change from *en-
jambed* lines to the "classical couplet." *Vers enjambe,*
or "overflow" verse, as it has been proposed to call
that style of versification in which the thought flows
loosely on through the verses to its natural close, is
the distinctive note of all romantic poetry.

The "classical couplet" restrains the lawlessness
and violence of intemperate verse by confining the
sense within the narrow boundaries of the distich.
The history of the change would involve an examination of the literary chronology of the seventeenth century.   It must be sufficient here to refer the student
to Edmund Waller and to George Sandys for the
earliest correct use of the couplet and to recommend
a comparison of Dryden's verse, in which the *enjambe-
ment* is often to be found, with the polished, perfected
couplets of Pope, unmixed with triplets, or Alexan-
drines, or *vers enjambe.* "Pope," says Professor
Saintsbury, "sacrifices every attraction of form to the
couplet — light, bright, glittering, varied in a manner
almost impossible to account for, tipped ever with the
neatest, smartest, sharpest rhyme, and volleying on
the dazzled, though at times at any rate satiated,
reader a sort of salvo of *feux-d'artifice*, skipping,
crackling, scattering color and sound all round and
about him.   If we take a paragraph of Milton's with

one of Pope's, and compare the apparent variety of
the constituent stones of the one building with the
apparent monotony of those of the other, the difference may be at first quite bewildering. One of Dryden's, between the two, will partly, though not
entirely, solve the difficulty by showing how the law
of the prose paragraph, that of meaning, is brought
to supply the place of that of the pure poetic paragraph, the composition of sound and music."

The reader of Pope will be struck by the conventional phraseology, and the evident artifice in the
choice of words. He is neither wayward in his verse,
nor unexpected in his phrase. His poetry is strictly
artificial, rhetorical, mundane. It exhibits the same
cold, glittering monotony, "like frosting round a
cake," says Mr. Lowell.

Neither poetry nor prose could long be confined
within the narrow limits appointed by the masters
of the classical vogue. The artificialities ceased, and
romanticism began again with Gray and Cowper, and
the eyes of poetry were again opened to the great
world, and men began to look curiously at the flower
they plucked, and hands were reached into the romantic past, and Percy collected his *Reliques of Ancient
English Poetry*, and prepared the way for Chatterton,
and for the *Lyrical Ballads*, and for greater things
beyond.

POPE'S PLACE IN LITERATURE

(From the *Life of Alexander Pope*, by W. J. Courthope,
pp. 353-357.)

The poetry of Pope occupies a central position
between two fluctuating movements of English taste.
The classical school of the eighteenth century, of
which he was the pioneer, was a protest against what
has been rightly called the metaphysical school of the
seventeenth century, just as the romantic school,
which arose in the early part of the present century,
was a reacting movement in art against the critical
principles of the classical school. We ought not to
regard the differing characteristics of these poetical
groups as so many isolated phænomena : each is bound
to the other by a historical connection, the full significance of which must be determined by reference to
the course of English poetry as a whole. In other
words, to appreciate the true meaning of the conflicts
respecting the principles of poetry that have divided,
and still divide, rival schools of criticism in this
country, it is necessary to investigate the origin of
the idea of Nature, which each party holds to be the
foundation of Art. . . .

Greek poetry, both in its practice and its theory,
was based on the direct imitation of nature; that is
to say, its subject-matter was, for the most part, de-

rived from its own mythology, and was presented in forms which, to a great extent, arose out of the popular and religious institutions underlying all Greek social life. From these purely natural forms Aristotle reasoned to general principles which, according to him, were the laws of the Art of Poetry. The Roman poets and critics, adopting Greek models, carried them into all countries in which Latin culture predominated, so that before the fall of the Roman empire what may be called a common sense of Nature, and common rules of rhetoric, prevailed wherever the art of poetry was practised in Europe.

The irruption of the barbarians obliterated like a deluge the landmarks of ancient criticism; the Latin language itself was only saved from destruction in the ark of the Christian Church. All the reasoning of Aristotle, Cicero, and Quintilian seemed, like the Roman empire itself, to have completely perished: for whole centuries the voice of poetry was silent in the Western World. In course of time new languages began to spring out of the decomposition of Latin, and, as was natural, their infancy was cradled in new forms of the poetic art. But the idea of Nature reflected in these forms was no longer one derived from direct imitation. A fresh conception of Man's relation to God, of the life beyond the grave, and, consequently, of the material universe, had come into being with the Christian Religion. And not only had Christianity supervened, but upon Christianity had been grafted Theology, and on Theology the Scholastic Philosophy. When we consider that the reappearance of Poetry is almost contemporaneous with the appearance of the Schoolmen, we can hardly doubt that much of the intellectual subtlety distinguishing the art of the Provençals was derived from the same atmosphere which inspired the five great doctors of the Mediæval Church. Other influences, no doubt, contributed largely to the creation of the new Idea of Nature. The prevalence of feudal institutions, the enthusiasm of the Crusades, the neighborhood of Oriental thought, represented by the Arabs in Spain, and by the philosophy of Averroes and Avicenna incorporated in Christian theology; all this, operating on minds learning to express themselves in novel forms of language, and unfettered by the critical principles of the ancient world, encouraged a new and vigorous growth of poetical conception. Hence the multitude of forms in which the poets of that early age manipulated what to us appears an extraordinary triviality of matter. Sirvente, Sonnet, Ballad, Virelay, Tenson, with all their subtle and scientific combinations of harmony, convey to us ideas of Nature far more shadowy than do the odes of Horace; nevertheless it is evident that for the audiences of the Middle Ages they possessed not only music, but warmth and meaning.

In time the mediæval idea of Nature ceased to commend itself to the general sense of Europe. The wars between Christian and Paynim ceased; the widespread system of Feudalism waned before the advance of centralizing Monarchy; the Reformation divided the Western World into two opposing camps; and, with the Balance of Power that began to emerge from the chaos, appeared the first rudiments of International Law. Yet so vigorous and trenchant were the forms of Mediæval Art, that they long survived the dissolution of the social conditions out of which they originally sprang. Dryden has well said that all poets have their family descents. And if anything is plain, it is that the poets of the seventeenth century, in the various countries of Europe, are directly and lineally descended from mediæval masters of the art. In Italy the long-lived family of the Petrarchists echoed faithfully, if monotonously, the music of their first ancestor; in Spain Cultorists and Conceptualists aimed at the same subtleties of thought and language that may be found in the original manner of the Troubadours; Voiture in France amused the society of the Hôtel Rambouillet with rondeau, ballad, and sonnet, the prototypes of which had helped to dispel the *ennui* of the feudal castle in the intervals of the Crusades; Saccharissas and Castaras in England emulated the fame of Beatrice and Laura; Quarles meditated his "Emblems," and Phineas Fletcher his "Purple Island," just as if the allegorical interpretation of Nature still held the field, and Bacon had not succeeded to the throne of St. Thomas Aquinas.

Meantime, however, the foundations of a new critical tradition were being silently laid. The old classical principle of the direct imitation of Nature, rising from its ashes, was everywhere reasserting its authority. We may fairly boast that the honor of having first revived the practice of this great principle belongs to an Englishman. Dante and Petrarch indeed show the influence of classical *forms* in their language, but the cast of their thought is purely mediæval: the earliest poem which embodies the genuine classical spirit is Chaucer's *Canterbury Tales*. Afterwards Ariosto applied the imitative principle, with the perfection of taste, in the *Orlando Furioso* and Cervantes in *Don Quixote:* it found among the French a dramatic exponent in Molière and a poetical critic in Boileau. In this country Shakespeare made his Hamlet commend the principle to the players; and Dryden gave it a new application in the historical portrait-painting of his "Absalom and Achitophel." But the English poet who first consciously recognized the value of the truth as a canon of criticism, and upheld it by a regular system of reasoning, was undoubtedly Pope.

THE HOMERIC POEMS

A national epic is found in the early literature of every people tracing their life and being back to a primitive civilization. The *Nibelungen Lied*, in German; the *Kalevala* in Finnish; the *Mahabharata* and *Ramayana* in Sanskrit, and the *Beowulf* in Old English are such epics. They embody the mythological and legendary ideas of the people among whom they originate; in sense and in metre they are indigenous. The Homeric poems — the *Iliad* and the *Odyssey* — are the greatest epics of the world, and they reflect the earliest features of Aryan civilization. Through all the ages these poems have retained their high place in the estimation of the world and have been the steadfast foundation of all culture. The secret of their hold upon humanity through their riches, beauty, and power has been well expressed in the ardent admiration of Henry Nelson Coleridge: —

"Greek — the shrine of the genius of the Old World; as universal as our race, as individual as ourselves; of infinite flexibility, of indefatigable strength, with the complication and the distinctness of Nature herself; to which nothing was vulgar, from

which nothing was excluded; speaking to the ear like
Italian, speaking to the mind like English; with
words like pictures, with words like the gossamer
film of the summer; at once the variety and pictu-
resqueness of Homer, the gloom and the intensity of
Æschylus; not compressed to the closest by Thucydides, not fathomed to the bottom by Plato, not
sounding with all its thunders, nor lit up with all
its ardors even under the Promethean touch of
Demosthenes."

The Homeric world as revealed in these ancient
documents of Hellenic life has been well described by
Professor Jebb in his "Introduction to Homer," and
from his account the following brief remarks are
drawn.

The earth, as it is conceived in Homer, is a large
flat disc surrounded by the great river Oceanus; of
the countries of the earth Homer knows only those
which are neighbor to the Ægean Sea — Greece and
Northwestern Asia Minor. The Greeks are called
Achæans, Argives, and Danai. "Achæan Argos"
denotes the whole, or a great part, of the Peloponnesus, and "Pelasgian Argos" indicates Thessaly.
Peloponnesus and Thessaly are names which do not
occur in Homer. Hellas denotes merely a district in
the region afterwards called Thessaly. The topog-
raphy of the Troad is more clearly marked. The

country afterwards called Lydia is "Mæonia," identified by the mention of Mount Tmolus. The islands
of Crete and Rhodes, Tenedos, Imbros, Samothrace,
Lesbos, and Lemnos are named. "To the north
there is a dim rumor of nomads who roam the plains
beyond the Thracian hills, living on the milk of their
mares; yet the name 'Sythian' is not found. To the
south there is a rumor of 'swart faces' (Æthiopes),
'remotest of men'; and of pigmies, who dwell hard
by the banks of the river Ocean" (Jebb). Egypt is
noticed only in a chance reference to Thebes. "Phœnician" occurs only once, and Tyre is not named at all.
Homer's government is a monarchy; the king (*Basileus*) rules by divine right; he is *Zeus-nurtured*, that
is, "upheld and enlightened by Zeus." The king is
leader in war, supreme judge, president of the council of elders and of the popular assembly. A demesne
is assigned to him from the public land, and he discharges functions of public hospitality. The rights
of the people rest upon judicial precedents which are
upheld by the king. In Homer there is no word for
law. The king convenes a council consisting of a
small number of elders, who determine upon the business of state. In the *Iliad* the council is composed
of a few prominent chiefs, or kings, who hold the
same relations to Agamemnon as local elders to a
local king.

The gods are near to men and are easily invoked by
prayer or placated by sacrifice. "The ties of the
family are sacred in every relation." The *Iliad* has
several pictures of pure and tender conjugal affection.
Slavery was the doom of prisoners of war. Slaves
were employed in the house or on the land, but there
were also free hired laborers.

Man in Homer wears a shirt, or tunic (*chiton*), and
a mantle (*chlaina*); woman wears a robe (*peplus*)
reaching to her feet, and girdled at the waist by a
zone. "On her head she sometimes wears a high, stiff
coif, over the middle of which passes a many-colored
twisted band, while a golden fillet glitters at the front.
Either from the *coif*, or directly from the crown of
the head, a veil falls over shoulders and back."

The chief articles of Homeric armor are the shield,
the greaves, the belt, the helmet, the spear, and the
sword. The shield was usually round and composed
of several layers of oxhide covered with ornamented
metal; the greaves were defensive panoply of leather
or soft metal wrapped completely about the leg.
"The most elaborate work of art in Homer is the
shield of Achilles. The central part of the shield
was adorned with representations of earth, heaven,
sea, sun, moon, and stars. The outer rim of the
shield represented the earth-girdling river, Oceanus.
Between the boss and the rim successive concentric

bands displayed various scenes of human life: a besieged city; a city at peace; ploughing; reaping; vintage; oxen attacked by lions; sheep at pasture in a glen; youths and maidens dancing."

.There is no reference in Homer to coined money. The ordinary measure of value is the ox; a female slave is worth four oxen, a suit of "golden" armor is worth a hundred.

The Homeric place of the dead is "the house of Hades." Between the earth and Hades is an intermediate region of gloom, called Erebus. Beyond Hades is Tartarus, the prison of the Titans.

The Homeric poems were publicly recited by rhapsodes as early as 600 B.C. And the poems are found at an early date diffused throughout the Greek world. At Athens there was a special ordinance, probably as old as 600 B.C., prescribing that Homer should be recited at the festival of the Great Panathenæa, once in every four years. The earliest reference to Homer in literature is in a lost poem of Callinus, who flourished about 690 B.C. Pausanias reports Callinus as believing Homer to be the author of an epic called *Thebais*. The earliest quotation from Homer is made by Simonides of Ceos, born 566 B.C., who quotes *Il.* VI. 148 as the utterance of "the man of Chios."

The editions of Homer in the Alexandrian Library were chiefly of two classes, those known by the names of individual editors and those known by the names of cities. When cited collectively the latter are called the civic editions. It is believed that the copies known to the Alexandrians rested upon an older *vulgate* text, the sources of which are unknown. Zenodotus, an Ephesian, librarian of the Alexandrian Museum, in the third century B.C., published a recension of Homer and a Homeric glossary. His pupil, Aristophanes of Byzantium, also published a recension of Homer. Aristarchus of Samothrace was a pupil of Aristophanes and succeeded him as librarian of the Alexandrian Library. He published two editions of the text of Homer. Professor Jebb notes three general aspects of his work: he carefully studied the Homeric usage of words, he gave full weight to manuscript authority, and he commented on the subject-matter of Homer. A rival school of Homeric interpretation sprang up at Pergamum in Mysia, where Crates, a contemporary of Aristarchus, and librarian of Pergamum, published Homeric commentaries. He is said to have been the champion of "anomaly" as Aristarchus was the champion of "analogy"; that is, the Alexandrian school, represented by Aristarchus, was essentially a school of accurate grammatical scholarship, and insisted upon the strict application of rules to the forms of words, while Crates dwelt more upon the exceptions.

The results of the inquiry into the ancient study of Homer warrant a general conclusion of the highest importance in regard to the whole existing text of Homer. In the words of Professor Jebb it is as follows: "The editions used by Aristarchus represented an older common text, or vulgate, and one of these editions was that of Antimachus (circ. 410 B.C.), in which the variations appear to have been only of the same small kind as in the rest. Hence there is the strongest reason for believing that the common text of 200 B.C. went back at least to the fifth century B.C. But Aristarchus caused no breach in the transmission of the common text. He made no wild conjecture or violent dislocations. He handed on what he had received, with such help towards exhibiting it in a purer form as careful collation and study could give; and so, with comparatively slight modifications, it descended to the age from which our MSS. date. Our common text, then, we may reasonably believe, is fundamentally the same as that which was known to Aristarchus; and therefore, in all probability, it rests on the same basis as the text which was read by Plato and Thucydides." (Jebb, *Introduction to Homer*, p. 102.)

Two questions must still be referred to: the historical basis of the story of the *Iliad* and the vexed problem of the authorship of the Homeric poems.

Concerning the first, Walter Leaf says, in the *Companion to the Iliad*, "The poem may give us a true picture of Achaian Greece and its civilization, and yet be no proof that the armies of Agamemnon fought beneath the walls of Troy. But here, again, the discoveries of recent years, and notably those of Schliemann at Hissarlik, have tended, on the whole, to confirm the belief that there is a historic reality behind the tale of Troy. Two things seem to be clearly made out, First, the Achaian empire was sufficiently powerful to collect a great armament and transport it across the seas for a distant war. Here, as in so many unexpected points, we get light from Egypt; for it seems to be made out that about 1500 B.C. the Achaians were allies of the Libyans in a great invasion of Egypt; possibly colonies of them were actually established there. If the Achaians could invade Egypt, there is no antecedent improbability in their invading Troas. Secondly, at the very point where tradition placed the city of Troy, there actually was a town of unknown antiquity and of considerable power. Thus two of the conditions, which have been gravely doubted previously, are now shown to have actually existed, and there is no *a priori* improbability, much less an impossibility, in such a Trojan expedition as the *Iliad* describes. But we can say positively — if indeed it is not sufficiently evident on the face of it — that the details of the Homeric story cannot possibly be historic. To take one main point, it is a fundamental assumption of the whole *Iliad* that the Greeks and Trojans are essentially one people in civilization and belief, in dress, manners, and language. Hardly here and there, as, for instance, in the polygamy of Priam, do we find traces of non-Greek habits. But this likeness cannot have existed between the inhabitants of Mykenai and Troy — the Troy of Hissarlik. The inhabitants of Hissarlik had a culture of their own, but it was entirely different from, and inferior to, that of Mykenai. The siege of Troy was a conflict of two races and two cultures with nothing in common. The description of it in the *Iliad* is purely imaginary — a poetic idealization of an event which can at most have been known by distant tradition. Even if Agamemnon and Achilles ever really lived, the *Iliad* can no more be taken as a proof that they fought before Troy, than the romances of the Middle Ages can prove that Charlemagne headed a crusade and fought before Jerusalem."

There have always been sceptics who have doubted the unity of composition of the *Iliad*. As early as 1689, Bentley's confidence was shaken by signs of serious tampering with the text of Homer. Wood's *Essay on the Genius of Homer*, first published in 1769, and reissued in Germany in 1773, reiterated Bentley's honest doubts. "Finally, in 1795, Wolf marched forth in complete mail, a sheaf of sceptical arrows rattling on his harness, all of which he pointed and feathered, giving by his learning, or by masculine sense, buoyancy to their flight, so as to carry them into every corner of literary Europe. Then began the row, — then the steam was mounted which has never since subsided, — and then opened upon Germany a career of scepticism which, from the very first, promised to be contagious." (De Quincey.) Without revolving the arguments contained in Wolf's *Prolegomena*, and the immense critical literature that has followed upon it, it may not be amiss to point out the order and relationship of the books of the *Iliad* according to the latest scholarship. The subject of the epic is the "Wrath of Achilles," and this main, or central story is contained in the following books: I. The Quarrel of Agamemnon and Achilles; XI. The Rout of the Greeks; XVI. The Exploits and Death of Patroklos; XXII. The Slaying of Hector.

The tale is not absolutely complete, for scattered fragments found in the intervening books are needed to round out the narrative. The first book is complete in itself: Zeus has promised to avenge Achilles and proceeds to bring the Greeks and Trojans into a pitched battle in order that the Greeks may be defeated. The way by which this is brought about is

described in the second book: Zeus sends a false dream
to Agamemnon to tell him that the hour of victory is
at hand, while to the Trojans he sends Iris with a
command to march at once into the plain.   The close
of Book XI. leaves the Greeks in a state of defeat
and flight, deprived of all their leaders except Aias,
who still remains to cover the retreat.   But àt the
beginning of Book XVI. we find him defending the
ships.   The intervening explanatory narrative is to
be found at the end of XV., which fits on to the end
of XI.   The interval between XVI. and XXII. is
more difficult to bridge.   Book XVI. has brought us
to the death of Patroklos.   In Book XXII. we have
Achilles in the full career of revenge.   The intermediate action is accounted for in the following
manner by Walter Leaf: "In the original story the
body of Patroklos was not saved at all; the bringing
of the news of his death to Achilles in the beginning
of XVIII., in some form or another, probably stood
in the oldest form of the poem, and was immediately
followed by the issuing of Achilles from the camp as
told at the end of XIX."

With splendid eloquence De Quincey describes the
character and argues the unity of this stupendous
story of the Wrath of Achilles: —

"Now, this unity is sufficiently secured if it should
appear that a considerable section of the *Iliad* — and

that section by far the most full of motion, of human
interest, of tragical catastrophe, and through which
runs, as the connecting principle, a character the
most brilliant, magnanimous, and noble, that pagan
morality could conceive — was, and must have been,
the work and conception of a single mind. Achilles
revolves through that section of the *Iliad* in a series
of phases, each of which looks forward and backward
to all the rest. He travels like the sun through his
diurnal course. We see him first of all rising upon
us as a princely councillor for the welfare of the
Grecian host. We see him atrociously insulted in
this office; yet, still, though a king, and unused to
opposition, and boiling with youthful blood, nevertheless controlling his passion, and retiring in clouded
majesty. Even thus, though having now so excellent
a plea for leaving the army, and though aware of the
early death that awaited him if he stayed, he disdains
to profit by the evasion. We see him still living in
the tented field, and generously unable to desert those
who had so insultingly deserted *him*. We see him in
a dignified retirement, fulfilling all the duties of religion, friendship, hospitality; and, like an accomplished man of taste, cultivating the arts of peace.
We see him so far surrendering his wrath to the
earnest persuasion of friendship, that he comes forth
at a critical moment for the Greeks to save them from

ruin. What are his arms? He has none at all.
Simply by his voice he changes the face of the battle.
He shouts, and nations fly from the sound. Never
but once again is such a shout recorded by a poet: —

> ' He call'd so loud, that all the hollow deep
> Of hell resounded.'

Who called? *That* shout was the shout of an arch-
angel. Next, we see him reluctantly allowing his
dearest friend to assume his own arms; the kindness
and the modesty of his nature forbidding him to suggest, that not the divine weapons, but the immortal
arm of the wielder had made them invincible. His
friend perishes. Then we see him rise in his noon-
tide wrath, before which no life could stand. The
frenzy of his grief makes him for a time cruel and
implacable. He sweeps the field of battle like a
monsoon. His revenge descends perfect, sudden,
like a curse from heaven. We now recognize the
goddess-born. This is his avatar — the incarnate
descent of his wrath. Had he moved to battle under
the ordinary impulses of Ajax, Diomed, and the other
heroes, we never could have sympathized or gone
along with so withering a course. We should have
viewed him as a 'scourge of God,' or fiend, born for
the tears of wives and the maledictions of mothers.
But the poet, before he would let him loose upon men,

creates for him a sufficient, or at least palliating, motive. In the sternest of his acts we read only the anguish of his grief. This is surely the perfection of art. At length the work of destruction is finished; but if the poet leaves him at this point, there would be a want of repose, and we should be left with a painful impression of his hero as forgetting the earlier humanities of his nature, and brought forward only for final exhibition in his terrific phases. Now, therefore, by machinery the most natural, we see this paramount hero travelling back within our gentler sympathies, and revolving to his rest like the vesper sun disrobed of his blazing terrors. We see him settling down to that humane and princely character in which he had been first exhibited; we see him relenting at the sight of Priam's gray hairs, touched with the sense of human calamity, and once again mastering his passion (grief now) as formerly he had mastered his wrath. He consents that his feud shall sleep; he surrenders the corpse of his capital enemy; and the last farewell chords of the poem rise with a solemn intonation from the grave of 'Hector, the tamer of horses'—that noble soldier who had so long been the column of his country, and to whom, in his dying moments, the stern Achilles had declared, but then in the middle career of his grief, that no honorable burial should ever be granted.

"Such is the outline of an Achilleis, as it might be
gathered from the *Iliad;* and for the use of schools
we are surprised that such a beautiful whole has not
long since been extracted. A tale more affecting by
its story and vicissitudes does not exist; and, after
this, who cares in what order the non-essential parts
of the poem may be arranged, or whether Homer was
their author? It is sufficient that one mind must
have executed this Achilleis, in consequence of its
intense unity. Every part implies every other part.
With such a model before him as this poem on the
wrath of Achilles, Aristotle could not carry his notions
of unity too high. And the unifying mind which
could conceive and execute the Achilleis — that is
what we mean by Homer. As well might it be said,
that the parabola described by a cannon-ball was in
one half due to a first discharge, and in the other
half to a second, as that one poet could lay the preparations for the passion and sweep of such a poem,
whilst another conducted it to a close. Creation does
not proceed by instalments: the steps of its revolution are not successive, but simultaneous; and the
last book of the Achilleis was undoubtedly conceived
in the same moment as the first.

"What effect such an Achilleis, abstracted from the
Iliad, would probably leave upon the mind, it happens
that we can measure by our own childish experience.

In Russell's *Ancient Europe,* a book much used in the last century, there is an abstract of the *Iliad,* which presents very nearly the outline of an Achilleis, such as we have supposed. The heroes are made to speak in a sort of stilted, or at least buskined language, not unsuited to youthful taste: and from the close convergement of the separate parts, the interest is condensed. This book, in our eighth year, we read. It was our first introduction to the 'Tale of Troy divine'; and we do not deceive ourselves in saying, that this memorable experience drew from us the first unselfish tears that ever we shed; and by the stings of grief which it left behind, demonstrated its own natural pathos." (De Quincey, *Homer and the Homeridæ.*)

SUGGESTIONS TO TEACHERS

As the *Iliad* is one of the world's great masterpieces, it is a book to live with, not to read once and have done with. It is a source of perpetual profit, inspiration, and delight. It discloses at the fiftieth reading beauties that were unseen at the first acquaintance. In Homer, as Frederic Harrison says, "alone of the poets, a national life is transfigured, wholly beautiful, complete, and happy; where care, doubt, decay, are as yet unborn. Here is a secular

Eden of the natural man — man not yet fallen or ashamed. . . . And yet how seldom do we find a friend spellbound over the Greek Bible of antiquity, whilst they wade through torrents of magazine quotations from a petty versifier of to-day, and in an idle vacation will graze, as contentedly as cattle in a fresh meadow, through the chopped straw of a circulating library. A generation which will listen to *Pinafore* for three hundred nights, and will read M. Zola's seventeenth romance, can no more read Homer than it could read a cuneiform inscription. It will read about Homer just as it will read about a cuneiform inscription, and will crowd to see a few pots which probably came from the neighborhood of Troy. But to Homer and the primeval type of heroic man in his simple joyousness the cultured generation is really dead, as completely as some spoiled beauty of the ballroom is blind to the bloom of the heather or the waving of the daffodils in a glade."

The first duty of the teacher is to stimulate a healthy love of reading and to kindle that inextinguishable love for literature which, Gibbon said, in words which are burned into the memory, he would not exchange for the wealth of the Indies. We should not be deceived by any solemn pedantry or shallow pedagogy into regarding the *joy* of literary study as a mere dilettante amusement. In the public schools there is a large class of boys who come from bare homes where books are unknown, and another large class whose imaginations have been inflamed by the dime dreadful, or the weekly story paper. The manliest of stories, the most heroic of tales of adventures by land or sea, are too tame or too slow for the appetite of one of these. He is callous to Dana or Melville; he thinks "Westward Ho!" "tiresomely dull." If only he can be beguiled into a love of reading, all other things become possible to him. Grammar he will learn best not from rules and principles, but as it is organized in thought and feeling in the great masters of expression; and he will unconsciously grow into a likeness with the company he keeps. He will enlarge his vocabulary with each book observingly read, and his tongue will unconsciously grow fluent and his pen more facile as he acquires, apparently without labor, the difficult art of expression.

Most of us, a shrewd observer has said, find that true sympathy with our classics begins only then when our academic study of them is wholly at an end. There is therefore at first no need of glossaries and commentaries, and the poem may be treated as an English poem, and read for the delight of the narrative. The tale of Troy should first be told, and, with the student's curiosity thus aroused, the reading of the text begun. No hint need be given, until the

Iliad is read and read again, of what modern scholarship has discovered concerning Homer. Least of all
need the child's imagination be disturbed by theories
of the authorship of the books, and all the din of con-
troversy raised by Wolf and his successors.

No disciple of Herbart ever evolved a more careful
plan of education, or method of pedagogic practice,
than that which Robert Browning drew concerning
this very poem, and which may be commended to the
thoughtful attention of both teacher and pupil.

DEVELOPMENT

> My Father was a scholar and knew Greek.
> When I was five years old, I asked him once
> " What do you read about ? "
>   " The Siege of Troy."
> " What is a siege, and what is Troy ? "
>   Whereat
> He piled up chairs and tables for a town,
> Set me a-top for Priam, called our cat
> — Helen, enticed away from home (he said)
> By wicked Paris, who couched somewhere close
> Under the footstool, being cowardly,
> But whom — since she was worth the pains, poor puss —
> Towzer and Tray — our dogs, the Atreidai, — sought
> By taking Troy to get possession of
> — Always when great Achilles ceased to sulk,
> (My pony in the stable) — forth would prance

And put to flight Hector — our page boy's self.
This taught me who was who and what was what :
So far I rightly understood the case
At five years old : a huge delight it proved
And still proves — thanks to that instructor sage
My Father, who knew better than turn straight
Learning's full flare on weak-eyed ignorance,
Or, worse yet, leave weak eyes to grow sand-blind,
Content with darkness and vacuity.

It happened, two or three years afterward,
That — I and playmates playing at Troy's Siege —
My Father came upon our make-believe.
" How would you like to read yourself the tale
Properly told, of which I gave you first
Merely such notion as a boy could bear?
Pope, now, would give you the precise account
Of what some day by dint of scholarship,
You'll hear — who knows? — from Homer's very mouth.
Learn Greek by all means, read the ' Blind Old Man,
Sweetest of singers ' — *tuphlos* which means ' blind,'
Hedistos which means ' sweetest.'   Time enough !
Try, anyhow, to master him some day ;
Until when, take what serves for substitute,
Read Pope, by all means ! "
                                        So I ran through Pope,
Enjoyed the tale — what history so true ?
Also attacked my Primer, duly drudged,
Grew fitter thus for what was promised next —
The very thing itself, the actual words,
When I could turn — say, Buttman to account.

Time passed, I ripened somewhat: one fine day,
"Quite ready for the *Iliad*, nothing less?
There's Heine, where the big books block the shelf:
Don't skip a word, thumb well the Lexicon!"

I thumbed well, and skipped nowise till I learned
Who was who, what was what, from Homer's tongue,
And there an end of learning.   Had you asked
The all-accomplished scholar, twelve years old,
"Who was it wrote the *Iliad?*" — what a laugh!
"Why, Homer, all the world knows: of his life
Doubtless some facts exist: it's everywhere:
We have not settled, though, his place of birth:
He begged, for certain, and was blind beside:
Seven cities claimed him — Scio, with best right,
Thinks Byron.   What he wrote?   Those Hymns we have.
Then there's the 'Battle of the Frogs and Mice,'
That's all — unless they dig 'Margites' up
(I'd like that) nothing more remains to know."

Thus did youth spend a comfortable time;
Until — "What's this the Germans say is fact
That Wolf found out first?   It's unpleasant work
Their chop and change, unsettling one's belief:
All the same, while we live, we learn, that's sure."
So, I bent brow o'er Prolegomena.

And, after Wolf, a dozen of his like
Proved there was never any Troy at all,
Neither Besiegers nor Besieged, — nay worse, —
No actual Homer, no authentic text,
No warrant for the fiction I, as fact,

Had treasured in my heart and soul so long —
Ay, mark you! and as fact held still, still hold,
Spite of new knowledge, in my heart of hearts
And soul of souls, fact's essence freed and fixed
From accidental fancy's guardian sheath. .
Assuredly thenceforth — thank my stars ! —
However it got there, deprive who could —
Wring from the shrine my precious tenantry,
Helen, Ulysses, Hector and his spouse,
Achilles and his friend ? — though Wolf — ah, Wolf !
Why must he needs come doubting, spoil a dream ?
But then, "No dream's worth waking" — Browning says :
And here's the reason why I tell thus much.
I, now mature man, you anticipate,
May blame my Father justifiably
For letting me dream out my nonage thus,
And only by such slow and sure degrees
Permitting me to sift the grain from chaff,
Get truth and falsehood known and named as such.
Why did he ever let me dream at all,
Not bid me taste the story in its strength ?
Suppose my childhood was scarce qualified
To rightly understand mythology,
Silence at least was in his power to keep :
I might have — somehow — correspondingly —
Well, who knows by what method, gained my gains,
Been taught, by forthrights, not meanderings,
My aim should be to loathe, like Peleus' son,
A lie as Hell's Gate, love my wedded wife,
Like Hector, and so on with all the rest.
Could not I have excogitated this
Without believing such men really were ?

That is — he might have put into my hand
The " Ethics " ?   In translation, if you please,
Exact, no pretty lying that improves,
To suit the modern taste: no more, no less —
The " Ethics " : 'tis a treatise I find hard
To read aright now that my hair is gray,
And I can manage the original.
At five years old — how ill had fared its leaves !
Now, growing double o'er the Stagirite,
At least I soil no page with bread and milk,
Nor crumple, dogs-ear and deface — boys' way.

The student will find the following books helpful in
the study of Pope and his translation of the *Iliad*: —
Robert Carruthers, *The Life of Alexander Pope*, London, 1857. C. W. Dilke, *Papers of a Critic*, 1875.
W. J. Courthope, *Life of Pope*, Vol. V. of Elwin's edition of Pope (Murray), 10 vols., 1871–1889. *The Iliad
of Homer; translated by Mr. Pope*, first four books,
1715; next three volumes, 1716, 1717, 1718; last two
volumes in 1720. Leslie Stephen, "Pope," in the series
of *English Men of Letters* (Harper), 1880. De Quincey, "Pope," in *Biographical Essays*. De Quincey,
Homer and the Homeridæ. Lowell, "Pope," in *My
Study Windows*. R. C. Jebb, *Introduction to the Iliad
and the Odyssey* (Ginn), 1887. Walter Leaf, *Companion to the Iliad* (Macmillan), 1892. G. C. W. Warr,
The Greek Epic (London), 1895. J. P. Mahaffy, *Social
Life in Greece from Homer to Menander* (Macmillan),
1874. Andrew Lang, *Homer and the Epic* (Long-
mans), 1893. Charles Mills Gayley, *Classic Myths in
English Literature* (Ginn), 1893.

POPE'S ILIAD

BOOK I

THE CONTENTION OF ACHILLES AND AGAMEMNON

ACHILLES'° wrath, to Greece the direful spring
Of woes unnumber'd, heav'nly goddess,° sing!
That wrath which hurl'd to Pluto's° gloomy reign°
The souls of mighty chiefs untimely slain;
Whose limbs,° unburied on the naked shore,   5
Devouring dogs and hungry vultures tore:
Since great Achilles and Atrides° strove,
Such° was the sov'reign doom, and such the will of
     Jove!
   Declare, O Muse! in what ill-fated hour
Sprung the fierce strife, from what offended power? 10
Latona's° son a dire contagion spread,
And heap'd the camp with mountains of the dead;
The king° of men his rev'rend° priest defied,
And, for the king's offence, the people died.

For Chryses sought with costly gifts to gain   15
His captive daughter from the victor's chain.
Suppliant the venerable father stands;
Apollo's awful ensigns grace his hands:
By these he begs; and, lowly bending down,
Extends the sceptre° and the laurel crown.   20
He sued to all, but chief implor'd for grace
The brother-kings of Atreus' royal race:
   "Ye° kings and warriors! may your vows be
      crown'd,
And Troy's proud walls lie level with the ground;
May Jove restore you, when your toils are o'er,   25
Safe to the pleasures of your native shore.
But oh! relieve a wretched parent's pain,
And give Chryseïs° to these arms again;
If mercy fail, yet let my presents move,
And dread avenging Phœbus,° son of Jove."   30
   The Greeks in shouts their joint assent declare,
The priest to rev'rence, and release the fair.°
Not so Atrides: he, with kingly pride,
Repuls'd the sacred sire, and thus replied:
   "Hence on thy life, and fly these hostile plains,   35
Nor ask, presumptuous, what the king detains;
Hence, with thy laurel crown and golden rod,
Nor trust too far those ensigns of thy god.

Mine is thy daughter, priest, and shall remain;
And prayers, and tears, and bribes, shall plead in
    vain; 40
Till time shall rifle every youthful grace,
And age dismiss her from my cold embrace;
In daily labours of the loom employ'd,
Or doom'd to deck the bed she once enjoy'd.
Hence then; to Argos° shall the maid retire, 45
Far from her native soil and weeping sire."
  The trembling priest along the shore return'd,
And in the anguish of a father mourn'd.
Disconsolate, not daring to complain,
Silent he wander'd° by the sounding main; 50
Till, safe at distance, to his god he prays,
The god who darts around the world his rays:
  "O Smintheus°! sprung from fair Latona's line,
Thou guardian power of Cilla° the divine,
Thou source of light! whom Tenedos adores, 55
And whose bright presence gilds thy Chrysa's shores;
If e'er with wreaths I hung thy sacred fane,
Or fed the flames with fat of oxen slain;
God of the silver bow! thy shafts employ,
Avenge° thy servant, and the Greeks destroy." 60
  Thus Chryses pray'd: the fav'ring power attends,
And from Olympus' lofty tops descends.°

Bent was his bow, the Grecian hearts to wound;
Fierce, as he mov'd, his silver shafts resound.
Breathing revenge, a sudden night he spread,   65
And gloomy darkness roll'd around° his head.
The fleet in view, he twang'd his deadly bow,
And hissing fly the feather'd fates below.
On mules and dogs th' infection first began;
And last, the vengeful arrows fix'd in man.   70
For nine long nights through all the dusky air
The pyres thick-flaming shot a dismal glare.
But ere the tenth revolving day was run,
Inspir'd by Juno,° Thetis'° god-like son
Conven'd to council all the Grecian train;   75
For much the goddess mourn'd her heroes slain.
   Th' assembly seated, rising o'er the rest,
Achilles thus the king of men address'd:
   "Why leave we not the fatal Trojan shore,
And measure back the seas we cross'd before?   80
The plague destroying whom the sword would spare,°
'Tis time to save the few remains of war.°
But let some prophet or some sacred sage
Explore the cause of great Apollo's rage;
Or learn the wasteful vengeance to remove   85
By mystic° dreams, for dreams descend from Jove.
If broken vows this heavy curse have laid,

Let altars smoke, and hecatombs° be paid.
So heav'n aton'd shall dying Greece restore,
And Phœbus dart his burning shafts no more." 90
  He said, and sate: when Calchas thus replied,
Calchas° the wise, the Grecian priest and guide,
That sacred seer, whose comprehensive view
The past, the present, and the future knew:
Uprising slow, the venerable sage 95
Thus spoke the prudence and the fears of age;
  "Belov'd of Jóve, Achilles! wouldst thou know
Why angry Phœbus bends his fatal bow?
First give thy faith, and plight a prince's word
Of sure protection, by thy pow'r and sword. 100
For I must speak what wisdom would conceal,
And truths invidious to the great reveal.
Bold is the task, when subjects, grown too wise,
Instruct a monarch where his error lies;
For though we deem the short-liv'd fury past, 105
'Tis sure, the mighty will revenge at last."
  To whom Pelides: "From thy inmost soul
Speak what thou know'st, and speak without control.
Ev'n by that god I swear, who rules the day,
To whom thy hands the vows of Greece convey, 110
And whose blest oracles thy lips declare:
Long as Achilles breathes this vital air,

No daring Greek, of all the num'rous band,
Against his priest shall lift an impious hand:
Not ev'n the chief by whom our hosts are led,   115
The king of kings, shall touch that sacred head."
    Encourag'd thus, the blameless° man replies:
"Nor vows unpaid, nor slighted sacrifice,
But he, our chief, provok'd the raging pest,
Apollo's vengeance for his injur'd priest.   120
Nor will the god's awaken'd fury cease,
But plagues shall spread, and fun'ral fires increase,
Till the great king, without a ransom paid,
To her own Chrysa send the black-ey'd° maid.
Perhaps, with added sacrifice and pray'r,   125
The priest may pardon, and the god may spare."
    The prophet spoke; when, with a gloomy frown,
The monarch started from his shining throne;
Black choler fill'd his breast that boil'd with ire,
And from his eyeballs flash'd the living fire.   130
"Augur accurs'd! denouncing mischief still,
Prophet of plagues, for ever boding ill!
Still must that tongue some wounding message bring,
And still thy priestly pride provoke thy king?
For this are Phœbus' oracles explor'd,   135
To teach the Greeks to murmur at their lord?
For this with falsehoods is my honour stain'd,

Is heaven offended, and a priest profan'd,
Because my prize, my beauteous maid, I hold,
And heav'nly charms prefer to proffer'd gold?   140
A maid, unmatch'd in manners as in face,
Skill'd in each art, and crown'd with every grace:
Not half so dear were Clytæmnestra's° charms,
When first her blooming beauties bless'd my arms.
Yet, if the gods demand her, let her sail;   145
Our cares are only for the public weal:
Let me be deem'd the hateful cause of all,
And suffer, rather than my people fall.
The prize, the beauteous prize, I will resign,
So dearly valu'd, and so justly° mine.   150
But since for common good I yield the fair,
My private loss let grateful Greece repair;
Nor unrewarded let your prince complain,
That he alone has fought and bled in vain."

 "Insatiate king!" (Achilles thus replies)   155
"Fond of the pow'r, but fonder of the prize!
Wouldst thou the Greeks their lawful prey should
     yield,
The due reward of many a well-fought° field?
The spoils of cities raz'd and warriors slain,
We share with justice, as with toil we gain: 160
But to resume whate'er thy av'rice craves

(That trick of tyrants) may be borne by slaves.
Yet if our chief for plunder only fight,
The spoils of Ilion shall thy loss requite,
Whene'er, by Jove's decree, our conqu'ring pow'rs 165
Shall humble to the dust her lofty tow'rs."
    Then thus the king: " Shall I my prize resign
With tame content, and thou possess'd of thine ?
Great as thou art, and like a god in fight,
Think not to rob me of a soldier's right.   170
At thy demand shall I restore the maid ?
First let the just equivalent be paid ;
Such as a king might ask ; and let it be
A treasure worthy her, and worthy me.
Or grant me this, or with a monarch's claim   175
This hand shall seize some other captive dame.
The mighty ° Ajax shall his prize resign,
Ulysses' spoils, or ev'n thy own, be mine.
The man who suffers, loudly may complain ;
And rage he may, but he shall rage in vain.   180
But this when time requires — it now remains
We launch a bark to plough the wat'ry plains,
And waft the sacrifice to Chrysa's shores,
With chosen pilots, and with lab'ring oars.
Soon shall the fair the sable ship ascend,   185
And some deputed prince the charge attend.

This Creta's° king, or Ajax shall fulfil,
Or wise Ulysses see perform'd our will;
Or, if our royal pleasure shall ordain,
Achilles' self conduct her o'er the main;   190
Let fierce Achilles, dreadful in his rage,
The god propitiate, and the pest assuage."
  At this, Pelides, frowning stern, replied:
" O tyrant, arm'd with insolence and pride!
Inglorious slave to int'rest, ever join'd   195
With fraud, unworthy of a royal mind!
What gen'rous Greek, obedient to thy word,
Shall form an ambush, or shall lift the sword?
What cause have I to war at thy decree?
The distant Trojans never injur'd me: 200
To Phthia's° realms no hostile troops they led;
Safe in her vales my warlike coursers fed;
Far hence remov'd, the hoarse-resounding main
And walls of rocks secure my native reign,
Whose fruitful soil luxuriant harvests grace,   205
Rich in her fruits, and in her martial race.
Hither we sail'd, a voluntary throng,
T' avenge a private, not a public wrong:
What else to Troy th' assembl'd nations draws,
But thine, ungrateful, and thy brother's cause?   210
Is this the pay our blood and toils deserve,

Disgrac'd and injur'd by the man we serve?
And dar'st thou threat to snatch my prize away,
Due to the deeds of many a dreadful day,
A prize as small, O tyrant, match'd with thine, 215
As thy own actions if compar'd to mine!
Thine in each conquest is the wealthy prey,
Though mine the sweat and danger of the day.
Some trivial present to my ships I bear,
Or barren praises pay the wounds of war. 220
But know, proud monarch, I'm thy slave no more;
My fleet shall waft me to Thessalia's shore.
Left by Achilles on the Trojan plain,
What spoils, what conquests, shall Atrides gain?"
  To this the king: " Fly, mighty warrior, fly! 225
Thy aid we need not and thy threats defy.
There want not chiefs in such a cause to fight,
And Jove himself shall guard a monarch's° right.
Of all the kings (the gods' distinguish'd care)
To pow'r superior none such hatred bear: 230
Strife° and debate thy restless soul employ,
And wars and horrors are thy savage joy.
If thou hast strength, 'twas heav'n that strength
    bestow'd,
For know, vain man! thy valour is from God.
Haste, launch thy vessels, fly with speed away, 235

Rule thy own realms with arbitrary sway:
I heed thee not, but prize at equal rate
Thy short-liv'd friendship and thy groundless hate.
Go, threat thy earth-born Myrmidons°; but here
'Tis mine to threaten, prince, and thine to fear.   240
Know, if the god the beauteous dame demand,
My bark shall waft her to her native land;
But then prepare, imperious prince! prepare,
Fierce as thou art, to yield thy captive fair:
Ev'n in thy tent I'll seize the blooming prize,   245
Thy lov'd Briseïs with the radiant eyes.
Hence shalt thou prove my might, and curse the hour
Thou stood'st a rival of imperial pow'r;
And hence to all our host it shall be known
That kings are subject to the gods alone."   250
   Achilles heard, with grief and rage oppress'd;
His heart swell'd high, and labour'd in his breast.
Distracting thoughts by turns his bosom rul'd,
Now fir'd by wrath, and now by reason cool'd:
That prompts his hand to draw the deadly sword,   255
Force thro' the Greeks, and pierce their haughty lord;
This whispers soft, his vengeance to control,
And calm the rising tempest of his soul.
Just as in anguish of suspense he stay'd,
While half unsheath'd appear'd the glitt'ring blade, 260

Minerva swift descended from above,
Sent by the sister and the wife of Jove
(For both the princes claim'd her equal care);
Behind she stood, and by the golden hair
Achilles seiz'd; to him alone confess'd,°   265
A sable cloud conceal'd her from the rest.
He sees, and sudden to the goddess cries,
Known by the flames that sparkle from her eyes:
  "Descends Minerva in her guardian care,
A heav'nly witness of the wrongs I bear   270
From Atreus' son?   Then let those eyes that view
The daring crime, behold the vengeance too."
  "Forbear!" (the progeny of Jove replies)
"To calm thy fury I forsake the skies:
Let great Achilles, to the gods resign'd,   275
To reason yield the empire o'er his mind.
By awful Juno this command is giv'n;
The king and you are both the care of heav'n.
The force of keen reproaches let him feel,
But sheath, obedient, thy revenging steel.   280
For I pronounce (and trust a heav'nly pow'r)
Thy injur'd honour has its fated hour,
When the proud monarch shall thy arms implore,
And bribe thy friendship with a boundless store.
Then let revenge no longer bear the sway,   285

Command thy passions, and the gods obey."
To her Pelides: "With regardful ear,
'Tis just, O goddess! I thy dictates hear.
Hard as it is, my vengeance I suppress:
Those who revere the gods, the gods will bless."　290
He said, observant of the blue-ey'd maid;
Then in the sheath return'd the shining blade.
The goddess swift to high Olympus flies,
And joins the sacred senate of the skies.

Nor yet the rage his boiling breast forsook,　295
Which thus redoubling on Atrides broke:
"O° monster! mix'd of insolence and fear,
Thou dog in forehead, but in heart a deer!
When wert thou known in ambush'd fights to dare,
Or nobly face the horrid front of war?　300
'Tis ours the chance of fighting fields to try;
Thine to look on and bid the valiant die.
So much 'tis safer thro' the camp to go,
And rob a subject, than despoil a foe.
Scourge of thy people, violent and base!　305
Sent in Jove's anger on a slavish race,
Who, lost to sense of gen'rous freedom past,
Are tam'd to wrongs, or this had been thy last.
Now by this sacred° sceptre hear me swear,
Which never more shall leaves or blossoms bear,　310

Which, sever'd from the trunk (as I from thee),
On the bare mountains left its parent tree;
This sceptre, form'd by temper'd steel to prove
An ensign of the delegates of Jove,
From whom the pow'r of laws° and justice springs 315
(Tremendous oath! inviolate to kings):
By this I swear, when bleeding Greece again
Shall call Achilles, she shall call in vain.
When, flush'd with slaughter, Hector comes to spread
The purpled shore with mountains of the dead,   320
Then shalt thou mourn th' affront thy madness gave,
Forc'd to deplore, when impotent to save:
Then rage in bitterness of soul, to know
This act has made the bravest Greek thy foe."

He spoke; and furious hurl'd against the ground 325
His sceptre starr'd with golden° studs around;
Then sternly silent sate.   With like disdain,
The raging king return'd his frowns again.

To calm their passion with the words of age,
Slow from his seat arose the Pylian sage,   330
Experienc'd Nestor,° in persuasion skill'd;
Words sweet as honey from his lips distill'd:
Two generations now had pass'd away,
Wise by his rules, and happy by his sway;
Two ages o'er his native realm he reign'd,   335

And now th' example of the third remain'd.
All view'd with awe the venerable man,
Who thus with mild benevolence began:
  "What shame, what woe is this to Greece! what joy
To Troy's proud monarch and the friends of Troy! 340
That adverse gods commit to stern debate
The best, the bravest, of the Grecian state.
Young as ye are, this youthful heat restrain,
Nor think your Nestor's years and wisdom vain.
A godlike race of heroes once I knew,   345
Such as no more these aged eyes shall view!
Lives there a chief to match Pirithous'° fame,
Dryas the bold, or Ceneus'° deathless name;
Theseus, endued with more than mortal might,
Or Polyphemus,° like the gods in fight?   350
With these of old to toils of battle bred,
In early youth my hardy days I led;
Fir'd with the thirst which virtuous envy breeds,
And smit with love of honourable deeds.
Strongest° of men, they pierc'd the mountain boar, 355
Rang'd the wild deserts red with monsters' gore,
And from their hills the shaggy Centaurs tore.
Yet these with soft persuasive arts I sway'd;
When Nestor spoke, they listen'd and obey'd.
If in my youth, ev'n these esteem'd me wise,   360

Do you, young warriors, hear my age advise.
Atrides, seize not on the beauteous slave;
That prize the Greeks by common suffrage gave:
Nor thou, Achilles, treat our prince with pride;
Let kings be just, and sov'reign pow'r preside.   365
Thee the first honours of the war adorn,
Like gods in strength and of a goddess born;
Him awful majesty exalts above
The pow'rs of earth and sceptred sons of Jove.
Let both unite with well-consenting mind,   370
So shall authority with strength be join'd.°
Leave me, O king! to calm Achilles' rage;
Rule thou thyself, as more advanc'd in age.
Forbid it, gods! Achilles should be lost,
The pride of Greece, and bulwark of our host."   375
   This said, he ceas'd; the king of men replies:
"Thy years are awful, and thy words are wise.
But that imperious, that unconquer'd soul,
No laws can limit, no respect control:
Before his pride must his superiors fall,   380
His word the law, and he the lord of all?
Him must our hosts, our chiefs, ourself obey?
What king can bear a rival in his sway?
Grant that the gods his matchless force have giv'n;
Has foul reproach a privilege from heav'n?"   385

Here on the monarch's speech Achilles broke,
And furious, thus, and interrupting, spoke:
"Tyrant, I well deserv'd thy galling chain,
To live thy slave, and still to serve in vain,
Should I submit to each unjust decree: 390
Command thy vassals, but command not me.
Seize on Briseïs, whom the Grecians doom'd
My prize of war, yet tamely see resum'd;
And seize secure; no more Achilles draws
His conqu'ring sword in any woman's cause. 395
The gods command me to forgive the past;
But let this first invasion be the last:
For know, thy blood, when next thou dar'st invade,
Shall stream in vengeance on my reeking blade."
   At this they ceas'd; the stern debate expir'd: 400
The chiefs in sullen majesty retir'd.
   Achilles with Patroclus took his way,
Where near his tents his hollow vessels lay.
Meantime Atrides launch'd with num'rous oars
A well-rigg'd ship for Chrysa's sacred shores: 405
High on the deck was fair Chryseïs plac'd,
And sage Ulysses with the conduct grac'd:
Safe in her sides the hecatomb they stow'd,
Then, swiftly sailing, cut the liquid road.
   The host to expiate next the king prepares, 410

c

With pure lustrations and with solemn pray'rs.
Wash'd by the briny ° wave, the pious train
Are cleans'd; and cast th' ablutions in the main.
Along the shores whole hecatombs were laid,
And bulls and goats to Phœbus' altars paid.   415
The sable fumes in curling spires arise,
And waft their grateful odours to the skies.
   The army thus in sacred rites engag'd,
Atrides still with deep resentment rag'd.
To wait his will two sacred heralds stood,   420
Talthybius ° and Eurybates ° the good.
" Haste to the fierce Achilles' tent," he cries,
" Thence bear Briseïs as our royal prize :
Submit he must; or, if they will not part,
Ourself in arms shall tear her from his heart."   425
   Th' unwilling heralds act their lord's commands;
Pensive they walk along the barren sands :
Arriv'd, the hero in his tent they find,
With gloomy aspect, on his arm reclin'd.
At awful distance long they silent stand,   430
Loth to advance or speak their hard command ;
Decent confusion !   This the godlike man
Perceiv'd, and thus with accent mild began :
   " With leave and honour enter our abodes,
Ye sacred ministers of men and gods !   435

I know your message; by constraint you came;
Not you, but your imperious lord, I blame.
Patroclus, haste, the fair Briseïs bring;
Conduct my captive to the haughty king.
But witness, heralds, and proclaim my vow,　　　440
Witness to gods above and men below!
But first and loudest to your prince declare,
That lawless tyrant whose commands you bear;
Unmov'd as death Achilles shall remain,
Tho' prostrate Greece should bleed at ev'ry vein:　445
The raging chief in frantic passion lost,
Blind to himself, and useless to his host,
Unskill'd to judge the future by the past,
In blood and slaughter shall repent at last."

　　Patroclus now th' unwilling beauty brought;　　450
She, in soft sorrows and in pensive thought,
Pass'd silent, as the heralds held her hand,
And oft look'd back, slow-moving o'er the strand.
　　Not so his loss the fierce Achilles bore;
But sad retiring to the sounding shore,　　　　455
O'er the wild margin of the deep he hung,
That kindred deep from whence his mother sprung;
There, bath'd in tears of anger and disdain,
Thus loud lamented to the stormy main:
　　"O parent° goddess! since in early bloom　　460

Thy son must fall, by too severe° a doom;
Sure, to so short a race of glory born,
Great Jove in justice should this span adorn.
Honour and fame at least the Thund'rer ow'd;
And ill he pays the promise of a god,   465
If yon proud monarch thus thy son defies,
Obscures my glories, and resumes my prize."
    Far in the deep recesses of the main,
Where aged ° Ocean holds his wat'ry reign,
The goddess-mother heard. The waves divide;   470
And like a mist she rose above the tide;
Beheld him mourning on the naked shores,
And thus the sorrows of his soul explores:
" Why grieves my son ? Thy anguish let me share,
Reveal the cause, and trust a parent's care."   475
    He, deeply sighing, said: "To tell my woe
Is but to mention what too well you know.
From Thebè,° sacred to Apollo's name,
Eëtion's ° realm, our conqu'ring army came,
With treasure loaded and triumphant spoils,   480
Whose just division crown'd the soldier's toils;
But bright Chryseïs, heav'nly prize! was led
By vote selected to the gen'ral's bed.
The priest of Phœbus sought by gifts to gain
His beauteous daughter from the victor's chain;   485

The fleet he reach'd, and, lowly bending down,
Held forth the sceptre and the laurel crown,
Entreating all; but chief implor'd for grace
The brother-kings of Atreus' royal race.
The gen'rous Greeks their joint consent declare,   490
The priest to rev'rence, and release the fair.
Not so Atrides: he, with wonted pride,
The sire insulted, and his gifts denied:
Th' insulted sire (his god's peculiar care)
To Phœbus pray'd, and Phœbus heard the pray'r: 495
A dreadful plague ensues; th' avenging darts
Incessant fly, and pierce the Grecian hearts.
A prophet then, inspir'd by heav'n, arose,
And points the crime, and thence derives the woes:
Myself the first th' assembled chiefs incline   500
T' avert the vengeance of the pow'r divine;
Then, rising in his wrath, the monarch storm'd;
Incens'd he threaten'd, and his threats perform'd:
The fair Chryseïs to her sire was sent,
With offer'd gifts to make the god relent;   505
But now he seiz'd Briseïs' heav'nly charms,
And of my valour's prize defrauds my arms,
Defrauds the votes of all the Grecian train;
And service, faith, and justice plead in vain.
But, goddess! thou thy suppliant son attend,   510

To high Olympus' shining court ascend,
Urge all the ties to former service ow'd,
And sue for vengeance to the thund'ring god.
Oft hast thou triumph'd in the glorious boast
That° thou stood'st forth, of all th' ethereal host,   515
When bold rebellion shook the realms above,
Th' undaunted guard of cloud-compelling Jove,
When the bright partner of his awful reign,
The warlike° maid, and monarch° of the main,
The traitor-gods, by mad ambition driv'n,   520
Durst threat with chains th' omnipotence of heav'n.
Then call'd by thee, the monster Titan came
(Whom gods Briareüs, men Ægeon name);
Through wand'ring skies enormous stalk'd along,
Not he that shakes the solid earth so strong: 525
With giant-pride at Jove's high throne he stands,
And brandish'd round him all his hundred hands.
Th' affrighted gods confess'd their awful lord,
They dropp'd the fetters, trembled and ador'd.
This, goddess, this to his rememb'rance call,   530
Embrace° his knees, at his tribunal fall;
Conjure him far to drive the Grecian train,
To hurl them headlong to their fleet and main,
To heap the shores with copious death, and bring
The Greeks to know the curse of such a king: 535

Let Agamemnon lift his haughty head
O'er all his wide dominion of the dead, ˙
And mourn in blood, that e'er he durst disgrace
The boldest warrior of the Grecian race."
    " Unhappy son ! " (fair Thetis thus replies,   540
While tears celestial trickle from her eyes)
" Why have I borne thee with a mother's throes,
To fates averse, and nurs'd for future woes ?
So short a space the light of heav'n to view !
So short a space ! and fill'd with sorrow, too !   545
Oh, might a parent's careful wish prevail,
Far, far from Ilion should thy vessels sail,
And thou, from camps remote, the danger shun,
Which now, alas ! too nearly threats my son ;
Yet (what I can) to move thy suit I'll go   550
To great Olympus crown'd with fleecy snow.
Meantime, secure within thy ships, from far
Behold the field, nor mingle in the war.
The sire of gods and all th' ethereal train
On the warm ° limits of the farthest main,   555
Now mix with mortals, nor disdain to grace
The feasts of Æthiopia's ° blameless race:
Twelve days the pow'rs indulge the genial rite,
Returning with the twelfth revolving light.
Then will I mount the brazen dome, and move   560

The high tribunal of immortal Jove."
　The goddess spoke: the rolling waves unclose;
Then down the deep she plung'd, from whence she
　　rose,
And left him sorrowing on the lonely coast,
In wild resentment for the fair he lost.   565
　In Chrysa's port now sage Ulysses rode;
Beneath the deck the destin'd victims stow'd;
The sails they furl'd, they lash'd the mast aside,
And dropp'd their anchors, and the pinnace tied.
Next on the shore their hecatomb they land,   570
Chryseis last descending on the strand.
Her, thus returning from the furrow'd main,
Ulysses led to Phœbus' sacred fane;
Where, at his solemn altar, as the maid
He gave to Chryses, thus the hero said: 575
　"Hail, rev'rend priest! to Phœbus' awful dome °
A suppliant I from great Atrides come:
Unransom'd here receive the spotless fair;
Accept the hecatomb the Greeks prepare;
And may thy god, who scatters darts around,   580
Aton'd by sacrifice, desist to wound."
　At this the sire embrac'd the maid again,
So sadly lost, so lately sought in vain.
Then near the altar of the darting king,

Dispos'd in rank their hecatomb they bring: 585
With° water purify their hands, and take
The sacred off'ring of the salted cake;
While thus, with arms devoutly rais'd in air,
And solemn voice, the priest directs his pray'r:
"God of the silver bow, thy ear incline, 590
Whose pow'r encircles Cilla the divine;
Whose sacred eye thy Tenedos surveys,
And gilds fair Chrysa with distinguish'd rays!
If, fir'd to vengeance at thy priest's request,
Thy direful darts inflict the raging pest; 595
Once more attend! avert the wasteful woe,
And smile propitious, and unbend thy bow."
So Chryses pray'd; Apollo heard his pray'r:
And now the Greeks their hecatomb prepare;
Between their horns the salted barley threw, 600
And with their heads to heav'n the victims slew:
The limbs they sever from th' inclosing hide;
The thighs, selected to the gods, divide:
On these, in double cauls involv'd with art,
The choicest morsels lay from ev'ry part. 605
The priest himself before his altar stands,
And burns the off'ring with his holy hands,
Pours the black wine, and sees the flame aspire;
The youths with instruments° surround the fire:

The thighs thus sacrific'd, and entrails dress'd,   610
Th' assistants part, transfix, and roast the rest:
Then spread the tables, the repast prepare,
Each takes his seat, and each receives his share.
When now the rage of hunger was repress'd,
With pure libations they conclude the feast;   615
The youths with wine the copious goblets crown'd,
And, pleas'd, dispense the flowing bowls around.
With hymns divine the joyous banquet ends,
The pæans° lengthen'd till the sun descends :
The Greeks, restor'd, the grateful notes prolong: 620
Apollo listens, and approves the song.
   'Twas night; the chiefs beside their vessel lie,
Till rosy morn had purpled o'er the sky :
Then launch, and hoise the mast; indulgent gales,
Supplied by Phœbus, fill the swelling sails;   625
The milk-white canvas bellying as they blow,
The parted ocean foams and roars below:
Above the bounding billows swift they flew,
Till now the Grecian camp appear'd in view.
Far on the beach they haul° their bark to land   630
(The crooked keel divides the yellow sand),
Then part, where, stretch'd along the winding bay,
The ships and tents in mingled prospect lay.
   But, raging still, amidst his navy sate

The stern Achilles, steadfast in his hate;   635
Nor mix'd in combat nor in council join'd;
But wasting cares lay heavy on his mind;
In his black thoughts revenge and slaughter roll,
And scenes of blood rise dreadful in his soul.   639
    Twelve days were past, and now the dawning light
The gods had summon'd to th' Olympian height:
Jove, first ascending from the wat'ry bow'rs,
Leads the long order of ethereal pow'rs.
When, like the morning mist, in early day,
Rose from the flood the daughter of the sea;   645
And to the seats divine her flight address'd.
There, far apart, and high above the rest,
The Thund'rer sate; where old Olympus shrouds
His hundred heads in heav'n and props the clouds.
Suppliant the goddess stood: one hand she plac'd   650
Beneath his beard, and one his knees embrac'd.
" If e'er, O father of the gods! " she said,
" My words could please thee, or my actions aid;
Some marks of honour on my son bestow,
And pay in glory what in life you owe.   655
Fame is at least by heav'nly promise due
To life so short, and now dishonour'd, too.
Avenge this wrong, O ever just and wise!
Let Greece be humbled, and the Trojans rise;

Till the proud king, and all th' Achaian race,   660
Shall heap with honours him they now disgrace."
   Thus Thetis spoke, but Jove in silence held
The sacred councils of his breast conceal'd.
Not so repuls'd, the goddess closer press'd,
Still grasp'd his knees, and urg'd the dear request. 665
"O sire of gods and men! thy suppliant hear;
Refuse, or grant; for what has Jove to fear?
Or, oh! declare, of all the pow'rs above,
Is wretched Thetis least the care of Jove?"
   She said, and sighing thus the god replies,   670
Who rolls the thunder o'er the vaulted skies:
   "What hast thou ask'd?   Ah! why should Jove
      engage   ✓
In foreign contests and domestic rage,
The gods' complaints, and Juno's fierce alarms,
While I, too partial, aid the Trojan arms?   675
Go, lest the haughty partner of my sway
With jealous eyes thy close access survey;
But part in peace, secure thy pray'r is sped:
Witness the sacred honours of our head,
The nod that ratifies the will divine,   680
The faithful, fix'd, irrevocable sign;
This seals thy suit, and this fulfils thy vows " —
He° spoke, and awful bends his sable brows,

Shakes his ambrosial curls, and gives the nod,
The stamp of fate, the sanction of the god :   685
High heav'n with trembling the dread signal took,
And all Olympus to the centre shook.

 Swift to the seas profound the goddess flies,
Jove to his starry mansion in the skies.
The shining synod of th' immortals wait   690
The coming god, and from their thrones of state
Arising silent, rapt in holy fear,
Before the majesty of heav'n appear.
Trembling they stand, while Jove assumes the throne,
All but the god's imperious queen alone :   695
Late had she view'd the silver-footed dame,
And all her passions kindled into flame.
" Say, artful manager of heav'n " (she cries),
" Who now partakes the secrets of the skies ?
Thy Juno knows not the decrees of fate,   700
In vain the partner of imperial state.
What fav'rite goddess then those cares divides,
Which Jove in prudence from his consort hides ? "

 To this the Thund'rer : " Seek not thou to find
The sacred counsels of almighty mind :   705
Involv'd in darkness lies the great decree,
Nor can the depths of fate be pierc'd by thee.
What fits thy knowledge, thou the first shalt know :

The first of gods above and men below;
But thou nor they shall search the thoughts that roll 710
Deep in the close recesses of my soul."
　Full on the sire, the goddess of the skies
Roll'd the large orbs of her majestic eyes,
And thus return'd : "Austere Saturnius,° say,
From whence this wrath, or who controls thy sway ? 715
Thy boundless will, for me, remains in force,
And all thy counsels take the destin'd course:
But 'tis for Greece I fear: for late was seen
In close consult° the silver-footed queen.
Jove to his Thetis nothing could deny,　　　　　720
Nor was the signal vain that shook the sky.
What fatal favour has the goddess won,
To grace her fierce inexorable son ?
Perhaps in Grecian blood to drench the plain,
And glut his vengeance with my people slain." 725
　Then thus the god: "Oh, restless fate of pride,
That strives to learn what heav'n resolves to hide!
Vain is the search, presumptuous and abhorr'd,
Anxious to thee and odious to thy lord.
Let this suffice; th' immutable decree　　　　730
No force can shake: what° is that ought to be.
Goddess, submit, nor dare our will withstand,
But dread the pow'r of this avenging hand;

Th' united strength of all the gods above
In vain resists th' omnipotence of Jove." 735
    The° Thund'rer spoke, nor durst the queen reply;
A rev'rend horror silenc'd all the sky.
The feast disturb'd, with sorrow Vulcan saw
His mother menac'd, and the gods in awe;
Peace at his heart, and pleasure his design, 740
Thus interpos'd the architect° divine:
"The wretched quarrels of the mortal state
Are far unworthy, gods! of your debate:
Let men their days in senseless strife employ;
We, in eternal peace and constant joy. 745
Thou, goddess-mother, with our sire comply,
Nor break the sacred union of the sky:
Lest, rous'd to rage, he shake the blest abodes,
Launch the red lightning, and dethrone the gods.
If you submit, the Thund'rer stands appeas'd. 750
The gracious pow'r is willing to be pleas'd."
    Thus Vulcan spoke; and, rising with a bound,
The double bowl with sparkling nectar crown'd,
Which held to Juno in a cheerful way,
"Goddess," he cried, "be patient and obey. 755
Dear as you are, if Jove his arm extend,
I can but grieve, unable to defend.
What god so daring in your aid to move,

Or lift his hand against the force of Jove ?
Once in your cause I° felt his matchless might,   760
Hurl'd headlong downward from th' ethereal height;
Toss'd all the day in rapid circles round;
Nor, till the sun descended, touch'd the ground:
Breathless I fell, in giddy motion lost;
The Sinthians° rais'd me on the Lemnian coast."   765
　He said, and to her hands the goblet heav'd,
Which, with a smile, the white-arm'd queen receiv'd.
Then to the rest he fill'd; and, in his turn,
Each to his lips applied the nectar'd urn.
Vulcan with awkward grace his office plies,   770
And unextinguish'd° laughter shakes the skies.
　Thus the blest gods the genial day prolong,
In feasts ambrosial and celestial song.
Apollo tun'd the lyre; the muses round
With voice alternate aid the silver sound.   775
Meantime the radiant sun, to mortal sight
Descending swift, roll'd down the rapid light.
Then to their starry domes the gods depart,
The shining monuments of Vulcan's art:
Jove on his couch reclin'd his awful head,   780
And Juno slumber'd on the golden bed.

BOOK VI

Now heav'n forsakes the fight; th' immortals yield
To human force and human skill the field:
Dark show'rs of jav'lins fly from foes to foes;
Now here, now there, the tide of combat flows;
While Troy's fam'd streams, that bound the deathful
    plain,   5
On either side run purple to the main.
  Great Ajax° first to conquest led the way,
Broke the thick ranks, and turn'd the doubtful day.
The Thracian Acamas his falchion° found,
And hew'd th' enormous giant to the ground;   10
His thund'ring arm a deadly stroke impress'd
Where the black horse-hair nodded o'er his crest:
Fix'd in his front the brazen weapon lies,
And seals in endless shades his swimming eyes.   14
  Next Teuthras' son distain'd the sands with blood,
Axylus,° hospitable, rich, and good:
In fair Arisbe's walls (his native place)

D   33

He held his seat; a friend to human race.
Fast by the road, his ever-open door
Oblig'd the wealthy, and reliev'd the poor.   20
To stern Tydides now he falls a prey,
No friend to guard him in the dreadful day!
Breathless the good man fell, and by his side
His faithful° servant, old Calesius, died.

By great Euryalus was Dresus slain,   25
And next he laid Opheltius on the plain.
Two twins were near, bold, beautiful, and young,
From a fair Naiad° and Bucolion sprung
(Laomedon's white flocks Bucolion fed,
That monarch's first-born by a foreign bed;   30
In secret woods he won the Naiad's grace,
And two fair infants crown'd his strong embrace):
Here dead they lay in all their youthful charms;
The ruthless victor stripp'd their shining arms.

Astyalus by Polypœtes fell;   35
Ulysses' spear Pidytes sent to hell°;
By Teucer's° shaft brave Aretaön bled,
And Nestor's° son laid stern Ablerus dead;
Great Agamemnon, leader of the brave,
The mortal wound of rich Elatus gave,   40
Who held in Pedasus° his proud abode,
And till'd the banks where silver Satnio flow'd.

Melanthius by Eurypylus was slain;
And Phylacus from Leitus flies in vain.
　Unbless'd Adrastus next at mercy lies　　45
Beneath the Spartan° spear, a living prize.
Scar'd with the din and tumult of the fight,
His headlong steeds, precipitate in flight,
Rush'd on a tamarisk's° strong trunk, and broke
The shatter'd chariot from the crooked yoke:　　50
Wide o'er the field, resistless as the wind,
For Troy they fly, and leave their lord behind.
Prone on his face he sinks beside the wheel:
Atrides o'er him shakes his vengeful steel;
The fallen chief in suppliant posture press'd　　55
The victor's knees, and thus his prayer address'd:
　"Oh, spare my youth, and for the life I owe
Large gifts of price my father shall bestow:
When fame shall tell that, not in battle slain,
Thy hollow ships his captive son detain,　　60
Rich heaps of brass shall in thy tent be told,°
And steel well-temper'd, and persuasive gold."
　He said: compassion touch'd the hero's heart
He stood suspended with the lifted dart:
As pity pleaded for his vanquish'd prize,　　65
Stern Agamemnon swift to vengeance flies,
And furious thus: "O impotent of mind!

Shall these, shall these Atrides' mercy find?
Well hast thou known proud Troy's perfidious land,
And well her natives merit at thy hand!   70
Not one of all the race, nor sex, nor age,
Shall save a Trojan from our boundless rage:
Ilion shall perish whole, and bury all;
Her babes, her infants at the breast, shall fall,
A dreadful lesson of exampled fate,   75
To warn the nations, and to curb the great."
   The monarch spoke; the words, with warmth ad-
    dress'd,
To rigid justice steel'd his brother's breast.
Fierce from his knees the hapless chief he thrust;
The monarch's jav'lin stretch'd° him in the dust.   80
Then, pressing with his foot his panting heart,
Forth from the slain he tugg'd the reeking dart.
Old Nestor saw, and rous'd the warriors' rage!
"Thus, heroes! thus the vig'rous combat wage!
No son of Mars descend, for servile gains,   85
To touch the booty, while a foe remains.
Behold yon glitt'ring host, your future° spoil!
First gain the conquest, then reward the toil."
   And now had Greece eternal fame acquir'd,
And frighted Troy within her walls retir'd;   90
Had not sage Helenus° her state redress'd,

Taught by the gods that mov'd his sacred breast:
Where Hector stood, with great Æneas join'd,
The seer reveal'd the counsels of his mind:
"Ye gen'rous chiefs! on whom th' immortals lay 95
The cares and glories of this doubtful day,
On whom your aids, your country's hopes depend,
Wise to consult, and active to defend!
Here, at our gates, your brave efforts unite,
Turn back the routed, and forbid the flight; 100
Ere yet their wives' soft arms the cowards gain,
The sport and insult of the hostile train.
When your commands have hearten'd every band,
Ourselves, here fix'd, will make the dang'rous stand;
Press'd as we are, and sore of former fight, 105
These straits demand our last remains of might.
Meanwhile, thou, Hector, to the town retire,
And teach our mother° what the gods require:
Direct the queen to lead th' assembled train
Of Troy's chief matrons to Minerva's fane; 110
Unbar the sacred gates, and seek the pow'r
With offer'd vows, in Ilion's topmost tow'r.
The largest mantle her rich wardrobes hold,
Most priz'd for art, and labour'd o'er with gold,
Before the goddess' honour'd knees be spread; 115
And twelve young heifers to her altars led.

If so the pow'r aton'd by fervent pray'r,
Our wives, our infants, and our city spare,
And far avert Tydides' wasteful ire,
That mows whole troops, and makes all Troy retire. 120
Not thus Achilles taught our hosts to dread,
Sprung tho' he was from more than mortal bed;
Not thus resistless rul'd the stream of fight,
In rage unbounded, and unmatch'd in might."

    Hector obedient heard; and, with a bound,   125
Leap'd from his trembling chariot to the ground;
Thro' all his host, inspiring force, he flies,
And bids the thunder of the battle rise.
With rage recruited the bold Trojans glow,
And turn the tide of conflict on the foe: 130
Fierce in the front he shakes two dazzling spears;
All Greece recedes, and midst her triumph fears:
Some god, they thought, who rul'd the fate of wars,
Shot down avenging, from the vault of stars.

    Then thus, aloud: " Ye dauntless Dardans, hear! 135
And you whom distant nations send to war;
Be mindful of the strength your fathers bore;
Be still yourselves and Hector asks no more.
One hour demands me in the Trojan wall,
To bid our altars flame, and victims fall: 140
Nor shall, I trust, the matrons' holy train

And rev'rend elders seek the gods in vain."
  This said, with ample strides the hero pass'd;
The shield's° large orb behind his shoulder cast,
His neck o'ershading, to his ancle hung;   145
And as he march'd the brazen buckler rung.
  Now paus'd the battle (godlike Hector gone),
When daring Glaucus° and great Tydeus' son
Between both armies met; the chiefs from far
Observ'd each other, and had mark'd° for war.   150
Near as they drew, Tydides thus began:
  "What art thou, boldest of the race of man?
Our eyes, till now, that aspect ne'er beheld,
Where fame is reap'd amid th' embattl'd field;
Yet far before the troops thou dar'st appear,   155
And meet a lance the fiercest heroes fear.
Unhappy they, and born of luckless sires,
Who tempt our fury when Minerva fires!
But if from heav'n, celestial thou descend,
Know, with immortals we no more contend.   160
Not long Lycurgus° view'd the golden light,
That daring man who mix'd with gods in fight;
Bacchus, and Bacchus' votaries, he drove
With brandish'd steel from Nyssa's sacred grove;
Their consecrated spears lay scatter'd round,   165
With curling vines and twisted ivy bound;

While Bacchus headlong sought the briny flood,
And Thetis' arms receiv'd the trembling god.
Nor fail'd the crime th' immortals' wrath to move
(Th' immortals bless'd with endless ease above);　170
Depriv'd of sight, by their avenging doom,
Cheerless he breath'd, and wander'd in the gloom:
Then sunk unpitied to the dire abodes,
A wretch accurs'd, and hated by the gods!
I brave not heav'n; but if the fruits of earth　175
Sustain thy life, and human be thy birth,
Bold as thou art, too prodigal of breath,
Approach, and enter the dark gates of death."

　"What, or from whence I am, or who my sire,"
Replied the chief, "can Tydeus' son enquire?　180
Like leaves on trees the race of man is found,
Now green in youth, now with'ring on the ground:
Another race the following spring supplies,
They fall successive, and successive rise;
So generations in their course decay,　185
So flourish these, when those are pass'd away.
But if thou still persist to search my birth,
Then hear a tale that fills the spacious earth:

　"A city stands on Argos' utmost bound
(Argos the fair, for warlike steeds renown'd);　190
Æolian° Sisyphus, with wisdom bless'd,

In ancient time the happy walls possess'd,
Then called Ephyre°: Glaucus was his son;
Great Glaucus, father of Bellerophon,
Who o'er the sons of men in beauty shin'd,   195
Lov'd for that valour which preserves mankind.
Then mighty Prœtus Argos' sceptre sway'd,
Whose hard commands Bellerophon obey'd.
With direful jealousy the monarch rag'd,
And the brave prince in num'rous toils engag'd.   200
For him, Antea° burn'd with lawless flame,
And strove to tempt him from the paths of fame:
In vain she tempted the relentless youth,
Endu'd with wisdom, sacred fear, and truth.
Fir'd at his scorn, the queen to Prœtus fled,   205
And begg'd revenge for her insulted bed:
Incens'd he heard, resolving on his fate;
But hospitable° laws restrain'd his hate:
To Lycia the devoted youth he sent,
With tablets° seal'd, that told his dire intent.   210
Now, bless'd by ev'ry pow'r who guards the good,
The chief arriv'd at Xanthus' silver flood:
There Lycia's monarch paid him honours due:
Nine days he feasted, and nine bulls he slew.
But° when the tenth bright morning orient glow'd,   215
The faithful youth his monarch's mandate show'd:

The fatal tablets, till that instant seal'd,
The deathful secret to the king reveal'd.
First, dire Chimæra's° conquest was enjoin'd;
A mingled monster, of no mortal kind;   220
Behind, a dragon's fiery tail was spread;
A goat's rough body bore a lion's head;
Her pitchy nostrils flaky flames expire;
Her gaping throat emits infernal fire.

 "This pest he slaughter'd (for he read the skies,   225
And trusted heav'n's informing prodigies°);
Then met in arms the Solymæan° crew
(Fiercest of men), and those the warrior slew.
Next the bold Amazons'° whole force defied;
And conquer'd still, for heav'n was on his side.   230

 "Nor ended here his toils: his Lycian foes,
At his return, a treach'rous ambush rose,
With levell'd spears along the winding shore:
There fell they breathless, and return'd no more.

 "At length the monarch with repentant grief   235
Confess'd the gods, and god-descended chief;
His daughter gave, the stranger to detain,
With half the honours of his ample reign.
The Lycians grant a chosen space of ground,
With woods, with vineyards, and with harvests crown'd.
There long the chief his happy lot possess'd,   241

With two brave sons° and one fair daughter° bless'd
(Fair ev'n in heav'nly eyes; her fruitful love
Crown'd with Sarpedon's birth th' embrace of Jove).
But when at last, distracted in his mind,   245
Forsook by heav'n, forsaking human kind,
Wide o'er th' Aleian° field he chose to stray,
A long, forlorn, uncomfortable way!
Woes heap'd on woes consum'd his wasted heart;
His beauteous daughter fell by Phœbe's° dart;   250
His eldest-born° by raging Mars was slain
In combat on the Solymæan plain.
Hippolochus surviv'd; from him I came,
The honour'd author of my birth and name;
By his decree I sought the Trojan town,   255
By his instructions learn to win renown;
To stand the first in worth as in command,
To add new honours to my native land;
Before my eyes my mighty sires to place,
And emulate the glories of our race."   260
    He spoke, and transport fill'd Tydides' heart;
In earth the gen'rous warrior fix'd his dart,
Then friendly, thus, the Lycian prince address'd:
"Welcome, my brave hereditary guest!
Thus ever let us meet with kind embrace,   265
Nor stain the sacred friendship of our race.

Know, chief, our grandsires have been guests of old,
Œneus the strong, Bellerophon the bold ;
Our ancient seat his honour'd presence grac'd,
Where twenty days in genial rites he pass'd.   270
The parting heroes mutual presents left;
A golden goblet was thy grandsire's gift;
Œneus a belt of matchless work bestow'd,
That rich with Tyrian° dye refulgent glow'd
(This from his pledge I learn'd, which, safely stor'd 275
Among my treasures, still adorns my board :
For Tydeus° left me young, when Thebe's wall
Beheld the sons of Greece untimely fall).
Mindful of this, in friendship let us join;
If heav'n our steps to foreign lands incline,   280
My guest in Argos thou, and I in Lycia thine.
Enough of Trojans to this lance shall yield,
In the full harvest of yon ample field;
Enough of Greeks shall dye thy spear with gore;
But thou and Diomed be foes no more.   285
Now change we arms, and prove to either host
We guard the friendship of the line we boast."
　　Thus having said, the gallant chiefs alight,
Their hands they join, their mutual faith they plight;
Brave Glaucus° then each narrow thought resign'd 290
(Jove warm'd his bosom and enlarg'd his mind);

For Diomed's brass arms, of mean device,
For which nine oxen paid (a vulgar price),
He gave his own, of gold divinely wrought;
A hundred beeves the shining purchase bought.   295
   Meantime the guardian of the Trojan state,
Great Hector, enter'd at the Scæan° gate.
Beneath the beech-trees'° consecrated shades,
The Trojan matrons and the Trojan maids
Around him flock'd, all press'd with pious care   300
For husbands, brothers, sons, engag'd in war.
He bids the train in long procession go,
And seek the gods, t' avert th' impending woe.
And now to Priam's stately courts he came,
Rais'd on arch'd columns of stupendous frame;   305
O'er these a range of marble structure runs;
The rich pavilions of his fifty sons,
In fifty chambers lodged: and rooms of state
Oppos'd to those, where Priam's daughters sate:
Twelve domes for them and their lov'd spouses shone,
Of equal beauty, and of polish'd stone.   311
Hither great Hector pass'd, nor pass'd unseen
Of royal Hecuba, his mother queen
(With her Laodice,° whose beauteous face
Surpass'd the nymphs of Troy's illustrious race).   315
Long in a strict embrace she held her son,

And press'd his hand, and tender thus begun :
  "O Hector !° say, what great occasion calls
My son from fight, when Greece surrounds our walls ?
Com'st thou to supplicate th' almighty pow'r,   320
With lifted hands from Ilion's lofty tow'r ?
Stay, till I bring the cup with Bacchus crown'd,
In Jove's high name, to sprinkle on the ground,
And pay due vows to all the gods around.
Then with a plenteous draught refresh thy soul,   325
And draw new spirits from the gen'rous bowl;
Spent as thou art with long laborious fight,
The brave defender of thy country's right."
  "Far° hence be Bacchus' gifts," the chief rejoin'd ;
"Inflaming wine, pernicious to mankind,   330
Unnerves the limbs, and dulls the noble mind.
Let chiefs abstain, and spare the sacred juice
To sprinkle to the gods, its better use.
By me that holy office were profan'd;
Ill fits it me, with human gore distain'd,   335
To the pure skies these horrid hands to raise,
Or offer heav'n's great sire polluted praise.
You, with your matrons, go, a spotless train !
And burn rich odours in Minerva's fane.
The largest mantle your full wardrobes hold,   340
Most priz'd for art, and labour'd o'er with gold,

Before the goddess' honour'd knees be spread,
And twelve young heifers to her altar led.
So may the pow'r, aton'd by fervent pray'r,
Our wives, our infants, and our city spare,   345
And far avert Tydides' wasteful ire,
Who mows whole troops, and makes all Troy retire.
Be this, O mother, your religious care;
I go to rouse soft Paris to the war;
If yet, not lost to all the sense of shame,   350
The recreant warrior hear the voice of fame.
Oh would kind earth the hateful wretch embrace,
That pest of Troy, that ruin of our race!
Deep to the dark abyss might he descend,
Troy yet should flourish, and my sorrows end."   355
   This heard, she gave command; and summon'd came
Each noble matron and illustrious dame.
The Phrygian queen to her rich wardrobe went,
Where treasur'd odours breath'd a costly scent.
There lay the vestures of no vulgar art,   360
Sidonian maids embroider'd ev'ry part,
Whom from soft Sidon° youthful Paris bore,
With Helen touching on the Tyrian shore.
Here as the queen revolv'd with careful eyes
The various textures and the various dyes,   365
She chose a veil that shone superior far,

And glow'd refulgent as the morning star.
Herself with this the long procession leads;
The train majestically slow proceeds.
Soon as to Ilion's topmost tow'r they come,   370
And awful reach the high Palladian° dome,
Antenor's consort, fair Theano,° waits
As Pallas' priestess, and unbars the gates.
With hands uplifted, and imploring eyes,
They fill the dome with supplicating cries.   375
The priestess then the shining veil displays,
Plac'd on Minerva's knees, and thus she prays:
  "O awful goddess! ever-dreadful maid,
Troy's strong defence, unconquer'd Pallas, aid!
Break thou Tydides' spear, and let him fall   380
Prone on the dust before the Trojan wall.
So twelve young heifers, guiltless of the yoke,
Shall fill thy temple with a grateful smoke.
But thou, aton'd by penitence and pray'r,
Ourselves, our infants, and our city spare!"   385
So pray'd the priestess in her holy fane;
So vow'd the matrons, but they vow'd in vain.
  While these appear before the pow'r with pray'rs,
Hector to Paris' lofty dome repairs.
Himself the mansion rais'd, from ev'ry part   390
Assembling architects of matchless art.

Near Priam's court and Hector's palace stands
The pompous structure, and the town commands.
A spear the hero bore of wond'rous strength,
Of full ten° cubits was the lance's length;   395
The steely point with golden ringlets° join'd,
Before him brandish'd, at each motion shin'd.
Thus ent'ring, in the glitt'ring rooms he found
His brother-chief, whose useless° arms lay round,
His eyes delighting with their splendid show,   400
Bright'ning the shield, and polishing the bow.
Beside him Helen with her virgins stands,
Guides their rich labours, and instructs° their hands.
    Him thus unactive, with an ardent look
The prince beheld, and high-resenting spoke: 405
"Thy hate to Troy is this the time to show
(O wretch ill-fated, and thy country's foe)?
Paris and Greece against us both conspire,
Thy close resentment, and their vengeful ire;
For thee great Ilion's guardian heroes fall,   410
Till heaps of dead alone defend her wall;
For thee the soldier bleeds, the matron mourns,
And wasteful war in all its fury burns.
Ungrateful man! deserves not this thy care,
Our troops to hearten, and our toils to share?   415
Rise, or behold the conqu'ring flames ascend,

E

And all the Phrygian glories at an end."
    "Brother, 'tis just," replied the beauteous youth,
" Thy free remonstrance proves thy worth and truth:
Yet charge my absence less, O gen'rous chief!   420
On hate to Troy, than conscious shame and grief.
Here, hid from human eyes, thy brother sate,
And mourn'd in secret his and Ilion's fate.
'Tis now enough: now glory spreads her charms,
And beauteous Helen calls her chief to arms.   425
Conquest to-day my happier sword may bless,
'Tis man's to fight, but heav'n's to give success.
But while I arm, contain thy ardent mind;
Or go, and Paris shall not lag behind."
    He said, nor answer'd Priam's warlike son;   430
When Helen thus with lowly grace begun:
" O gen'rous brother! if the guilty dame
That caus'd these woes deserve a sister's name!
Would heav'n, ere all these dreadful deeds were done,
The day that show'd me to the golden sun   435
Had seen my death! Why did not whirlwinds bear
The fatal infant to the fowls of air?
Why sunk I not beneath the whelming tide,
And midst the roarings of the waters died?
Heav'n fill'd up all my ills, and I accurs'd   440
Bore all, and Paris of those ills the worst.

Helen at least a braver spouse might claim,
Warm'd with some virtue, some regard of fame!
Now, tir'd with toils, thy fainting limbs recline,
With toils sustain'd for Paris' sake and mine:⁣ 445
The gods have link'd our miserable doom,
Our present woe and infamy to come:
Wide shall it spread, and last thro' ages long,
Example sad! and theme of future song."
    The chief replied: "This time forbids to rest: 450
The Trojan bands, by hostile fury press'd,
Demand their Hector, and his arm require;
The combat urges, and my soul's on fire.
Urge thou thy knight to march where glory calls,
And timely join me, ere I leave the walls. 455
Ere yet I mingle in the direful fray,
My wife, my infant, claim a moment's stay:
This day (perhaps the last that sees me here)
Demands a parting word, a tender tear:
This day some god, who hates our Trojan land, 460
May vanquish Hector by a Grecian hand."
    He said, and pass'd with sad-presaging heart,
To seek his spouse, his soul's far dearer part;
At home he sought her, but he sought in vain:
She, with one maid of all her menial train, 465
Had thence retir'd; and with her second° joy,

The young Astyanax,° the hope of Troy,
Pensive she stood on Ilion's tow'ry height,
Beheld the war, and sicken'd at the sight;
There her sad eyes in vain her lord explore,   470
Or weep the wounds her bleeding country bore.
   But he who found not whom his soul desir'd,
Whose virtue charm'd him as her beauty fir'd,
Stood in the gates, and ask'd what way she bent
Her parting step; if to the fane she went,   475
Where late the mourning matrons made resort;
Or sought her sisters in the Trojan court.
"Not to the court," replied th' attendant train,
"Nor, mix'd with matrons, to Minerva's fane:
To Ilion's steepy tow'r she bent her way,   480
To mark the fortunes of the doubtful day.
Troy fled, she heard, before the Grecian sword:
She heard, and trembled for her distant lord;
Distracted with surprise, she seem'd to fly,
Fear on her cheek, and sorrow in her eye.   485
The nurse attended with her infant boy,
The young Astyanax, the hope of Troy."
   Hector, this heard, return'd without delay;
Swift thro' the town he trod his former way,
Thro' streets of palaces and walks of state;   490
And° met the mourner at the Scæan gate.

With haste to meet him sprung the joyful fair,
His blameless wife, Eëtion's wealthy heir
(Cilician Thebe great Eëtion sway'd,
And Hippoplacus' wide-extended shade):   495
The nurse stood near, in whose embraces press'd,
His only hope hung smiling at her breast,
Whom each soft charm and early grace adorn,
Fair as the new-born star that gilds the morn.
To this lov'd infant Hector gave the name   500
Scamandrius, from Scamander's honour'd stream:
Astyanax the Trojans call'd the boy,
From his great father, the defence of Troy.
Silent the warrior smil'd, and, pleas'd, resign'd
To tender passions all his mighty mind: 505
His beauteous princess cast a mournful look,
Hung on his hand, and then dejected spoke;
Her bosom labour'd with a boding sigh,
And the big tear stood trembling in her eye.
"Too daring prince! ah whither dost thou run?   510
Ah too forgetful of thy wife and son!
And think'st thou not how wretched we shall be,
A widow I, a helpless orphan he!
For sure such courage length of life denies,
And thou must fall, thy virtue's sacrifice.   515
Greece in her single heroes strove in vain;

Now hosts oppose thee, and thou must be slain!
Oh grant me, gods! ere Hector meets his doom,
All I can ask of heav'n, an early tomb!
So shall my days in one sad tenour run,   520
And end with sorrows as they first begun.
No parent now remains, my griefs to share,
No father's aid, no mother's tender care.
The fierce Achilles wrapt° our walls in fire,
Laid Thebe waste, and slew my warlike sire!   525
His fate compassion in the victor bred;
Stern as he was, he yet rever'd the dead,
His radiant arms preserv'd from hostile spoil,
And laid him decent on the fun'ral pile;
Then rais'd a mountain where his bones were burn'd; 530
The mountain nymphs the rural tomb adorn'd;
Jove's sylvan daughters bade their elms bestow
A barren shade, and in his honour grow.
    "By the same arm my sev'n brave brothers fell;
In one sad day beheld the gates of hell;   535
While the fat herds and snowy flocks they fed,
Amid their fields the hapless heroes bled!
My mother liv'd to bear the victor's bands,
The queen of Hippoplacia's° sylvan lands:
Redeem'd too late, she scarce beheld again   540
Her pleasing empire and her native plain,

When, ah! oppress'd by life-consuming woe,
She fell a victim to Diana's bow.
  "Yet while my Hector still survives, I see
My father, mother, brethren, all, in thee.   545
Alas! my parents, brothers, kindred, all,
Once more will perish if my Hector fall.
Thy wife, thy infant, in thy danger share;
Oh prove a husband's and a father's care!
That quarter most the skilful Greeks annoy,   550
Where yon wild fig-trees join the wall of Troy:
Thou, from this tow'r defend th' important post;
There Agamemnon points his dreadful host,
That pass Tydides, Ajax, strive to gain,
And there the vengeful Spartan fires his train.   555
Thrice our bold foes the fierce attack have giv'n,
Or led by hopes, or dictated from heav'n.
Let others in the field their arms employ,
But stay my Hector here, and guard his Troy."
  The chief replied: "That post shall be my care,   560
Nor that alone, but all the works of war.
How would the sons of Troy, in arms renown'd,
And Troy's proud dames, whose garments sweep the
    ground,
Attaint the lustre of my former name,
Should Hector basely quit the field of fame?   565

My early youth was bred to martial pains,
My soul impels me to th' embattl'd plains :
Let me be foremost to defend the throne,
And guard my father's glories, and my own.
Yet come it will, the day decreed by fates   570
(How my heart trembles while my tongue relates !) ;
The day when thou, imperial Troy ! must bend,
And see thy warriors fall, thy glories end.
And yet no dire presage so wounds my mind,
My mother's death, the ruin of my kind,   575
Not Priam's hoary hairs defil'd with gore,
Not all my brothers gasping on the shore ;
As thine, Andromache ! thy griefs I dread ;
I see thee trembling, weeping, captive led !
In Argive looms our battles to design,   580
And woes of which so large a part was thine !
To bear the victor's hard commands, or bring
The weight of waters from Hyperia's° spring.
There, while you groan beneath the load of life,
They cry, 'Behold the mighty Hector's wife !'   585
Some haughty Greek, who lives thy tears to see,
Embitters all thy woes by naming me.
The thoughts of glory past, and present shame,
A thousand griefs, shall waken at the name !
May I lie cold before that dreadful day,   590

Press'd with a load of monumental clay!
Thy Hector, wrapp'd in everlasting sleep,
Shall neither hear thee sigh, nor see thee weep."
  Thus having spoke, th' illustrious chief of Troy
Stretch'd his fond arms to clasp the lovely boy.   595
The babe clung crying to his nurse's breast,
Scar'd at the dazzling helm, and nodding crest.
With secret pleasure each fond parent smil'd,
And Hector hasted to relieve his child;
The glitt'ring terrors from his brows unbound,   600
And placed the beaming helmet on the ground.
Then kiss'd the child, and, lifting high in air,
Thus to the gods preferr'd a father's pray'r:
  "O thou whose glory fills th' ethereal throne,
And all ye deathless powers! protect my son!   605
Grant him, like me, to purchase just renown,
To guard the Trojans, to defend the crown,
Against his country's foes the war to wage,
And rise the Hector of the future age!
So when, triumphant from successful toils,   610
Of heroes slain he bears the reeking spoils,
Whole hosts may hail him with deserv'd acclaim,
And say, 'This chief transcends his father's fame':
While pleas'd, amidst the gen'ral shouts of Troy,
His mother's conscious heart o'erflows with joy."   615

He spoke, and fondly gazing on her charms,
Restor'd the pleasing burthen to her arms;
Soft on her fragrant breast the babe she laid,
Hush'd to repose, and with a smile survey'd.
The troubled pleasure soon chastis'd by fear,   620
She mingled with the smile a tender tear.
The soften'd chief with kind compassion view'd,
And dried the falling drops, and thus pursu'd:
"Andromache! my soul's far better part,
Why with untimely sorrows heaves thy heart?   625
No hostile hand can antedate my doom,
Till fate condemns me to the silent tomb.
Fix'd is the term to all the race of earth,
And such the hard condition of our birth.
No force can then resist, no flight can save;   630
All sink alike, the fearful and the brave.
No more — but hasten to thy tasks at home,
There guide the spindle, and direct the loom:
Me glory summons to the martial scene;
The field of combat is the sphere for men.   635
Where heroes war, the foremost place I claim,
The first in danger as the first in fame."
Thus having said, the glorious chief resumes
His tow'ring helmet, black with shading plumes.
His princess parts with a prophetic sigh,   640

Unwilling parts, and oft reverts her eye,
That stream'd at ev'ry look : then, moving slow,
Sought her own palace, and indulg'd her woe.
There, while her tears deplor'd the godlike man,
Thro' all her train the soft infection ran ;   645
The pious maids their mingled sorrows shed,
And mourn the living Hector as the dead.

But now, no longer deaf to honour's call,
Forth issues Paris from the palace wall.
In brazen arms that cast a gleamy ray,   650
Swift thro' the town the warrior bends his way.
The wanton courser thus, with reins unbound,
Breaks from his stall, and beats the trembling ground;
Pamper'd and proud he seeks the wonted tides,
And laves, in height of blood, his shining sides :   655
His head now freed he tosses to the skies;
His mane dishevell'd o'er his shoulders flies;
He snuffs the females in the distant plain,
And springs, exulting, to his fields again.
With equal triumph, sprightly, bold, and gay,   660
In arms refulgent as the god of day,
The son of Priam, glorying in his might,
Rush'd forth with Hector to the fields of fight.
And now the warriors passing on the way,
The graceful Paris first excus'd his stay.   665

To whom the noble Hector thus replied:
" O chief! in blood, and now in arms, allied!
Thy pow'r in war with justice none contest;
Known is thy courage, and thy strength confess'd.
What pity, sloth should seize a soul so brave,   670
Or godlike Paris live a woman's slave!
My heart weeps blood at what the Trojans say,
And hopes thy deed shall wipe the stain away.
Haste then, in all their glorious labours share;
For much they suffer, for thy sake, in war.   675
These° ills shall cease, whene'er by Jove's decree
We crown the bowl to Heav'n and Liberty:
While the proud foe his frustrate triumphs mourns,
And Greece indignant thro' her seas returns."

BOOK XXII

THE DEATH OF HECTOR

Thus to their bulwarks, smit with panic fear,
The herded Ilians rush like driven deer;
There safe, they wipe the briny drops away,
And drown in bowls the labours of the day.
Close to the walls, advancing o'er the fields,   5
Beneath one roof° of well-compacted shields,
March, bending on, the Greeks' embodied pow'rs,
Far-stretching in the shade of Trojan tow'rs.
Great Hector singly stay'd; chain'd down by fate,
There fix'd he stood before the Scæan gate;   10
Still his bold arms determin'd to employ,
The guardian still of long-defended Troy.
   Apollo now to tir'd Achilles turns
(The pow'r confess'd in all his glory burns),
" And what," he cries, " has Peleus' son in view,   15
With mortal speed a godhead to pursue?
For not to thee to know the gods is giv'n,
Unskill'd to trace the latent marks of heav'n.

What boots thee now that Troy forsook the plain?
Vain thy past labour, and thy present vain: 20
Safe in their walls are now her troops bestow'd,
While here thy frantic rage attacks a god."
     The chief incens'd: " Too partial god of day!
To check my conquests in the middle way:
How few in Ilion else had refuge found!   25
What gasping numbers now had bit the ground!
Thou robb'st me of a glory justly mine,
Pow'rful of godhead, and of fraud divine:
Mean fame, alas! for one of heav'nly strain,
To cheat a mortal who repines° in vain."   30
     Then to the city, terrible and strong,
With high and haughty steps he tower'd along:
So the proud courser, victor of the prize,
To the near goal with double ardour flies.
Him, as he blazing shot across the field,   35
The careful eyes of Priam first beheld.
Not half so dreadful rises to the sight,
Thro' the thick gloom of some tempestuous night,
Orion's° dog (the year when autumn weighs),
And o'er the feebler stars exerts his rays;   40
Terrific glory! for his burning breath
Taints the red air with fevers, plagues, and death.
So flam'd his fiery mail.   Then° wept the sage:

He strikes his rev'rend head, now white with age;
He lifts his wither'd arms; obtests° the skies;   45
He calls his much-lov'd son with feeble cries:
The son, resolv'd Achilles' force to dare,
Full at the Scæan gate expects the war:
While the sad father on the rampart stands,
And thus adjures him with extended hands: 50
   "Ah stay not, stay not! guardless and alone
Hector, my lov'd, my dearest, bravest son!
Methinks already I behold thee slain,
And stretch'd beneath that fury of the plain.
Implacable Achilles! might'st thou be   55
To all the gods no dearer than to me!
Thee vultures wild should scatter round the shore,
And bloody dogs grow fiercer from thy gore!
How many valiant sons I late enjoy'd,
Valiant in vain! by thy curs'd arm destroy'd.   60
Or, worse than slaughter'd, sold in distant isles
To shameful bondage and unworthy toils.
Two, while I speak, my eyes in vain explore,
Two from one mother° sprung, my Polydore
And lov'd Lycaon; now perhaps no more!   65
Oh! if in yonder hostile camp they live,
What heaps of gold, what treasures would I give
(Their grandsire's wealth, by right of birth their own,

Consign'd his daughter with Lelegia's° throne):
But if (which heav'n forbid) already lost,   70
All pale they wander on the Stygian° coast,
What sorrows then must their sad mother know,
What anguish I! unutterable woe!
Yet less that anguish, less to her, to me,
Less to all Troy, if not depriv'd of thee.   75
Yet shun Achilles! enter yet the wall;
And spare thyself, thy father, spare us all!
Save thy dear life: or if a soul so brave
Neglect that thought, thy dearer glory save.
Pity, while yet I live, these silver hairs;   80
While yet thy father feels the woes he bears,
Yet curs'd with sense! a wretch, whom in his rage
(All trembling on the verge of helpless age)
Great Jove has plac'd, sad spectacle of pain!
The bitter dregs of fortune's cup to drain: 85
To fill with scenes of death his closing eyes,
And number all his days by miseries!
My heroes slain, my bridal bed o'erturn'd,
My daughters ravish'd, and my city burn'd,
My bleeding infants dash'd against the floor;   90
These I have yet to see, perhaps yet more!
Perhaps ev'n I, reserv'd by angry fate
The last sad relic of my ruin'd state

(Dire pomp of sov'reign wretchedness!), must fall
And stain the pavement of my regal hall;⁣   95
Where famish'd dogs, late guardians of my door,
Shall lick their mangled master's spatter'd gore.
Yet for my sons I thank ye, gods! 'twas well:
Well that they perish'd, for in fight they fell.
Who dies in youth and vigour, dies the best,   100
Struck thro' with wounds, all honest on the breast.
But when the fates, in fulness of their rage,
Spurn the hoar head of unresisting age,
In dust the rev'rend lineaments deform,
And pour to dogs the life-blood scarcely warm;   105
This, this is misery! the last, the worst,
That man can feel: man, fated to be curs'd!"

    He said, and acting what no words could say,
Rent from his head the silver locks away.
With him the mournful mother bears a part: 110
Yet all their sorrows turn not Hector's heart:
The zone° unbrac'd, her bosom she display'd;
And thus, fast-falling the salt tears, she said:

    "Have mercy on me, O my son! revere
The words of age; attend a parent's pray'r!   115
If ever thee in these fond arms I press'd,
Or still'd thy infant clamours at this breast;
Ah! do not thus our helpless years forego,

F

But, by our walls secur'd, repel the foe.
Against his rage if singly thou proceed,   120
Shouldst thou (but heav'n avert it!), shouldst thou
    bleed,
Nor must thy corse lie honour'd on the bier,
Nor spouse, nor mother, grace thee with a tear;
Far from our pious rites, those dear remains
Must feast the vultures on the naked plains."   125
    So they, while down their cheeks the torrents roll:
But fix'd remains the purpose of his soul;
Resolv'd he stands, and with a fiery glance
Expects the hero's terrible advance.
So, roll'd up in his den, the swelling snake   130
Beholds the traveller approach the brake;
When, fed with noxious herbs, his turgid veins
Have gather'd half the poisons° of the plains;
He burns, he stiffens with collected ire,
And his red eyeballs glare with living fire.   135
Beneath a turret, on his shield reclin'd,
He stood, and question'd thus his mighty mind:
    "Where° lies my way? To enter in the wall?
Honour and shame th' ungen'rous thought recall:
Shall° proud Polydamas before the gate   140
Proclaim his counsels are obey'd too late,
Which timely follow'd but the former night,

What numbers had been sav'd by Hector's flight?
That wise advice rejected with disdain,
I feel my folly in my people slain.   145
Methinks my suff'ring country's voice I hear,
But most, her worthless sons insult my ear,
On my rash courage charge the chance of war,
And blame those virtues which they cannot share.
No — if I e'er return, return I must   150
Glorious, my country's terror laid in dust:
Or if I perish, let her see me fall
In field at least, and fighting for her wall.
And yet suppose these measures I forego,
Approach unarm'd, and parley with the foe,   155
The warrior-shield, the helm, and lance lay down,
And treat on terms° of peace to save the town:
The wife° withheld, the treasure ill-detain'd
(Cause of the war, and grievance of the land),
With honourable justice to restore;   160
And add half Ilion's yet remaining store,
Which Troy shall, sworn, produce; that injur'd Greece
May share our wealth, and leave our walls in peace.
But why this thought? Unarm'd if I should go,
What hope of mercy from this vengeful foe,   165
But woman-like to fall, and fall without a blow?
We greet not here as man conversing man,

Met at an oak or journeying o'er a plain;
No season now for calm, familiar talk,
Like youths and maidens in an ev'ning walk :   170
War is our business, but to whom is giv'n
To die or triumph, that determine heav'n!"
    Thus pond'ring, like a god the Greek drew nigh:
His dreadful plumage nodded from on high;
The Pelian° jav'lin, in his better hand,   175
Shot trembling rays that glitter'd o'er the land;
And on his breast the beamy splendours shone
Like Jove's own light'ning, or the rising sun.
As Hector sees, unusual terrors rise,
Struck by some god, he fears, recedes,° and flies: 180
He leaves the gates, he leaves the walls behind;
Achilles follows like the winged wind.
Thus at the panting dove the falcon flies
(The swiftest racer of the liquid skies);
Just when he holds, or thinks he holds, his prey,   185
Obliquely wheeling thro' th' aërial way,
With open beak and shrilling cries he springs,
And aims his claws, and shoots upon his wings:
No less fore-right° the rapid chase they held,
One urg'd by fury, one by fear impell'd;   190
Now circling round the walls their course maintain,
Where the high watch-tow'r overlooks the plain;

Now where the fig-trees° spread their umbrage broad
(A wider compass), smoke along the road.
Next by Scamander's double source they bound,   195
Where two fam'd fountains burst the parted ground:
This hot thro' scorching clefts is seen to rise,
With exhalations steaming to the skies;
That the green banks in summer's heat o'erflows,
Like crystal clear, and cold as winter snows.   200
Each gushing fount a marble° cistern fills,
Whose polish'd bed receives the falling rills;
Where Trojan dames (ere yet alarm'd by Greece)
Wash'd their fair garments in the days of peace.
By these they pass'd, one chasing, one in flight   205
(The mighty fled, pursu'd by stronger might);
Swift was the course; no vulgar prize they play,
No vulgar victim must reward the day
(Such as in races crown the speedy strife):
The prize contended was great Hector's life.   210
   As when some hero's fun'rals are decreed,
In grateful honour of the mighty dead;
Where high rewards the vig'rous youth inflame
(Some golden tripod, or some lovely dame),
The panting coursers swiftly turn the goal,   215
And with them turns the rais'd spectator's soul:
Thus three times round the Trojan wall they fly;

The gazing gods lean forward from the sky:
To whom, while eager on the chase they look,
The sire of mortals and immortals spoke: 220
    "Unworthy sight! the man belov'd of heav'n,
Behold, inglorious round yon city driv'n!
My heart partakes the gen'rous Hector's pain;
Hector, whose zeal whole hecatombs has slain,
Whose grateful fumes the gods receiv'd with joy,   225
From Ida's summits and the tow'rs of Troy:
Now see him flying! to his fears resign'd,
And Fate and fierce Achilles close behind.
Consult, ye pow'rs ('tis worthy your debate),
Whether to snatch him from impending fate,   230
Or let him bear, by stern Pelides slain
(Good as he is), the lot impos'd on man?"
    Then Pallas thus: "Shall he whose vengeance
        forms
The forky bolt, and blackens heav'n with storms,
Shall he prolong one Trojan's forfeit breath,   235
A man, a mortal, pre-ordain'd to death?
And will no murmurs fill the courts above?
No gods indignant blame their partial Jove?"
    "Go then," return'd the sire, "without delay;
Exert thy will: I give the fates their way."   240
Swift at the mandate pleas'd Tritonia° flies,

And stoops impetuous from the cleaving skies.
  As thro' the forest, o'er the vale and lawn,
The well-breath'd beagle drives the flying fawn;
In vain he tries the covert of the brakes,   245
Or deep beneath the trembling thicket shakes:
Sure of the vapour° in the tainted dews,
The certain hound his various maze pursues:
Thus step by step, where'er the Trojan wheel'd,
There swift Achilles compass'd round the field.   250
Oft as to reach the Dardan° gates he bends,
And hopes th' assistance of his pitying friends
(Whose show'ring arrows, as he cours'd below,
From the high turrets might oppress the foe),
So oft Achilles turns him to the plain: 255
He eyes the city, but he eyes in vain.
As° men in slumbers seem with speedy pace
One to pursue, and one to lead the chase,
Their sinking limbs the fancied course forsake,
Nor this can fly, nor that can overtake: 260
No less the lab'ring heroes pant and strain;
While that but flies, and this pursues, in vain.
  What god, O Muse! assisted Hector's force,
With fate itself so long to hold the course!
Phœbus it was: who, in his latest hour,   265
Endu'd his knees with strength, his nerves with pow'r.

And great Achilles, lest some Greek's advance
Should snatch the glory from his lifted lance,
Sign'd to the troops, to yield his foe the way,
And leave untouch'd the honours of the day.   270
 Jove lifts the golden balances, that show
The fates of mortal men and things below:
Here each contending hero's lot he tries,
And weighs, with equal hand, their destinies.
Low sinks the scale surcharg'd with Hector's fate;   275
Heavy with death it sinks, and hell° receives the
  weight.
 Then Phœbus left him.   Fierce Minerva flies
To stern Pelides, and, triumphing, cries:
"O lov'd of Jove! this day our labours cease,
And conquest blazes with full beams on Greece.   280
Great Hector falls; that Hector fam'd so far,
Drunk with renown, insatiable of war,
Falls by thy hand and mine! nor force nor flight
Shall more avail him, nor his god of light.
See, where in vain he supplicates above,   285
Roll'd at the feet of unrelenting Jove!
Rest here: myself will lead the Trojan on,
And urge to meet the fate he cannot shun."
 Her voice divine the chief with joyful mind
Obey'd; and rested, on his lance reclin'd;   290

While like Deïphobus° the martial dame
(Her face, her gesture, and her arms, the same),
In show° an aid, by hapless Hector's side
Approach'd,° and greets him thus with voice belied :
   "Too long, O Hector! have I borne the sight   295
Of this distress, and sorrow'd in thy flight :
It fits us now a noble stand to make,
And here, as brothers, equal fates partake."
   Then he : "O prince! allied in blood and fame,
Dearer than all that own a brother's name;   300
Of all that Hecuba to Priam bore,
Long tried, long lov'd; much lov'd, but honour'd
     more!
Since you of all our num'rous race alone
Defend my life, regardless of your own."
   Again the goddess : "Much my father's pray'r,   305
And much my mother's, press'd me to forbear :
My friends embrac'd my knees, adjur'd my stay,
But stronger love impell'd, and I obey.
Come then, the glorious conflict let us try,
Let the steel sparkle and the jav'lin fly;   310
Or let us stretch Achilles on the field,
Or to his arm our bloody trophies yield."
   Fraudful she said; then swiftly march'd before;
The Dardan hero shuns his foe no more.

Sternly they met.   The silence Hector broke;   315
His dreadful plumage nodded as he spoke:
  "Enough, O son of Peleus!   Troy has view'd
Her walls thrice circled, and her chief pursu'd.
But now some god within me bids me try
Thine or my fate: I kill thee or I die.   320
Yet on the verge of battle let us stay,
And for a moment's space suspend the day:
Let heav'n's high pow'rs be call'd to arbitrate
The just conditions of this stern debate
(Eternal witnesses of all below,   325
And faithful guardians of the treasur'd vow!):
To them I swear: if, victor in the strife,
Jove by these hands shall shed thy noble life,
No vile dishonour shall thy corse pursue;
Stripp'd of its arms alone (the conqu'ror's due),   330
The rest to Greece uninjur'd I'll restore:
Now plight thy mutual oath, I ask no more."
  "Talk not of oaths," the dreadful chief replies,
While anger flash'd from his disdainful eyes,
" Detested as thou art, and ought to be,   335
Nor oath nor pact Achilles plights with thee;
Such pacts as lambs and rabid wolves combine,
Such leagues as men and furious lions join,
To such I call the gods! one constant state

Of lasting rancour and eternal hate :   340
No thought but rage, and never-ceasing strife,
Till death extinguish rage, and thought and life.
Rouse then thy forces this important hour,
Collect thy soul, and call forth all thy pow'r.
No farther subterfuge, no farther chance ;   345
'Tis Pallas, Pallas gives thee to my lance.
Each Grecian ghost by thee depriv'd of breath,
Now hovers round, and calls° thee to thy death."
  He spoke, and launch'd his jav'lin at the foe ;
But Hector shunn'd the meditated blow :   350
He stoop'd, while o'er his head the flying spear
Sung innocent, and spent its force in air.
Minerva watch'd it falling on the land,
Then drew, and gave to great Achilles' hand,
Unseen of Hector, who, elate with joy,   355
Now shakes his lance, and braves the dread of Troy :
  "The life you boasted to that jav'lin giv'n,
Prince ! you have miss'd. My fate depends on heav'n.
To thee (presumptuous as thou art) unknown
Or what must prove my fortune or thy own.   360
Boasting is but an art, our fears to blind,
And with false terrors sink another's mind.
But know, whatever fate I am to try,
By no dishonest wound shall Hector die ;

I shall not fall a fugitive at least,   365
My soul shall bravely issue from my breast.
But first, try thou my arm; and may this dart
End all my country's woes, deep buried in thy heart!"
    The weapon flew, its course unerring held;
Unerring, but the heav'nly shield repell'd   370
The mortal dart; resulting with a bound
From off the ringing orb, it struck the ground.
Hector beheld his jav'lin fall in vain,
Nor other lance nor other hope remain;
He calls Deïphobus, demands a spear,   375
In vain, for no Deïphobus was there.
All comfortless he stands; then, with a sigh:
" 'Tis so — heav'n wills it, and my hour is nigh!
I deem'd Deïphobus had heard my call,
But he secure lies guarded in the wall.   380
A god deceiv'd me; Pallas, 'twas thy deed:
Death and black fate approach! 'Tis I must bleed.
No refuge now, no succour from above,
Great Jove deserts me, and the son of Jove,
Propitious once and kind! Then welcome fate!   385
'Tis true I perish, yet I perish great:
Yet in a mighty deed I shall expire,
Let future ages hear it, and admire!"
    Fierce, at the word, his weighty sword he drew,

And, all collected, on Achilles flew.   390
So Jove's° bold bird, high balanc'd in the air,
Stoops from the clouds to truss the quiv'ring hare.
Nor less Achilles his fierce soul prepares;
Before his breast the flaming shield he bears,
Refulgent orb! above his fourfold° cone   395
The gilded horse-hair sparkled in the sun,
Nodding at ev'ry step (Vulcanian° frame!),
And as he mov'd, his figure seem'd on flame.
As radiant Hesper shines with keener light,
Far-beaming o'er the silver host of night,   400
When all the starry train emblaze the sphere:
So shone the point of great Achilles' spear.
In his right hand he waves the weapon round,
Eyes the whole man, and meditates the wound:
But° the rich mail Patroclus lately wore,   405
Securely cas'd the warrior's body o'er.
One place at length he spies, to let in fate,
Where 'twixt the neck and throat the jointed plate
Gave entrance: thro' that penetrable part
Furious he drove the well-directed dart: 410
Nor pierc'd the windpipe yet, nor took the pow'r
Of speech, unhappy! from thy dying hour.
Prone on the field the bleeding warrior lies,
While thus, triumphing, stern Achilles cries:

"At last is Hector stretch'd upon the plain,   415
Who fear'd no vengeance for Patroclus slain :
Then, prince! you should have fear'd what now you
    feel ;
Achilles absent was Achilles still.
Yet a short space the great avenger stay'd,
Then low in dust thy strength and glory laid.   420
Peaceful he sleeps, with all our rites adorn'd,
For ever honour'd, and for ever mourn'd :
While, cast to all the rage of hostile pow'r,
Thee birds shall mangle, and the dogs devour."
    Then Hector, fainting at th' approach of death :   425
"By thy own soul! by those who gave thee breath !
By all the sacred prevalence of pray'r ;
Ah, leave me not for Grecian dogs to tear !
The common rites of sepulture bestow,
To soothe a father's and a mother's woe ;   430
Let their large gifts procure an urn at least,
And Hector's ashes in his country rest."
    "No, wretch accurs'd !" relentless he replies
(Flames, as he spoke, shot flashing from his eyes),
"Not those who gave me breath should bid me spare,
Nor all the sacred prevalence° of pray'r.   436
Could I myself the bloody banquet join !
No — to° the dogs that carcase I resign.

Should Troy to bribe me bring forth all her store,
And, giving thousands, offer thousands more;   440
Should Dardan Priam, and his weeping dame,
Drain their whole realm to buy one fun'ral flame;
Their Hector on the pile they should not see,
Nor rob the vultures of one limb of thee."
   Then thus the chief his dying accents drew: 445
"Thy rage, implacable! too well I knew:
The Furies that relentless breast have steel'd,
And curs'd thee with a heart that cannot yield.
Yet think, a day will come, when fate's decree
And angry gods shall wreak this wrong on thee;   450
Phœbus and Paris shall avenge my fate,
And stretch° thee here, before this Scæan gate."
   He ceas'd: the fates suppress'd his lab'ring breath,
And his eyes stiffen'd at the hand of death;
To the dark realm the spirit wings its way   455
(The manly body left a load of clay),
And plaintive glides along the dreary coast,
A naked, wand'ring, melancholy ghost!
   Achilles, musing as he roll'd his eyes
O'er the dead hero, thus (unheard) replies: 460
"Die thou the first! when Jove and heav'n ordain,
I follow thee." He said, and stripp'd the slain.
Then, forcing backward from the gaping wound

The reeking jav'lin, cast it on the ground.
The thronging Greeks behold, with wond'ring eyes,   465
His manly° beauty and superior size:
While some, ignobler, the great dead deface°
With wounds ungen'rous, or with taunts disgrace.
"How chang'd that Hector! who, like Jove, of late
Sent lightning on our fleets and scatter'd fate!"   470
     High o'er the slain the great Achilles stands,
Begirt with heroes and surrounding bands;
And thus aloud, while all the host attends:
"Princes and leaders! countrymen and friends!
Since now at length the pow'rful will of heav'n   475
The dire destroyer to our arm has giv'n,
Is not Troy fall'n already?   Haste, ye pow'rs!
See if already their deserted tow'rs
Are left unmann'd; or if they yet retain
The souls of heroes, their great Hector slain.   480
But what is Troy, or glory what to me?
Or why reflects my mind on aught but thee,
Divine Patroclus! Death has seal'd his eyes;
Unwept, unhonour'd, uninterr'd he lies!
Can his dear image from my soul depart,   485
Long as the vital spirit moves my heart?
If, in the melancholy shades below,
The flames of friends and lovers cease to glow,

Yet mine shall sacred last; mine, undecay'd,
Burn on thro' death, and animate my shade. 490
Meanwhile, ye sons of Greece, in triumph bring
The corse of Hector, and your pæans sing.
Be this the song, slow moving tow'rd the shore,
'Hector° is dead, and Ilion is no more.'"

Then his fell soul a thought of vengeance bred 495
(Unworthy of himself, and of the dead);
The nervous ancles bor'd, his feet he bound
With thongs inserted thro' the double wound;
These fix'd up high behind the rolling wain,
His graceful head was trail'd along the plain. 500
Proud on his car th' insulting victor stood,
And bore aloft his arms, distilling blood.
He smites the steeds; the rapid chariot flies;
The sudden clouds of circling dust arise.
Now lost is all that formidable air; 505
The face divine and long-descending hair
Purple the ground, and streak the sable sand;
Deform'd, dishonour'd, in his native land!
Giv'n to the rage of an insulting throng!
And, in his parent's sight, now dragg'd along! 510

The mother first beheld with sad survey;
She rent her tresses, venerably grey,
And cast far off the regal veils away.

G

With piercing shrieks his bitter fate she moans,
While the sad father answers groans with groans; 515
Tears after tears his mournful cheeks o'erflow,
And the whole city wears one face of woe:
No less than if the rage of hostile fires,
From her foundations curling to her spires,
O'er the proud citadel at length should rise, 520
And the last blaze send Ilion to the skies.
The wretched monarch of the falling state,
Distracted, presses to the Dardan gate:
Scarce the whole people stop his desp'rate course,
While strong affliction gives the feeble force: 525
Grief tears his heart, and drives him to and fro,
In all the raging impotence of woe.
At length he roll'd in dust, and thus begun,
Imploring all, and naming one by one:
"Ah! let me, let me go where sorrow calls; 530
I, only I, will issue from your walls
(Guide or companion, friends! I ask ye none),
And bow before the murd'rer of my son;
My grief perhaps his pity may engage;
Perhaps at least he may respect my age. 535
He has a father, too; a man like me;
One not exempt from age and misery
(Vig'rous no more, as when his young embrace

Begot this pest of me and all my race).
How many valiant sons, in early bloom,   540
Has that curs'd hand sent headlong to the tomb!
Thee, Hector! last; thy loss (divinely brave!)
Sinks my sad soul with sorrow to the grave.
Oh had thy gentle spirit pass'd in peace,
The son expiring in the sire's embrace,   545
While both thy parents wept thy fatal hour,
And, bending o'er thee, mix'd the tender show'r!
Some comfort that had been, some sad relief,
To melt in full satiety of grief!"

   Thus wail'd the father, grov'ling on the ground,   550
And all the eyes of Ilion stream'd around.

   Amidst her matrons Hecuba appears
(A mourning princess, and a train in tears):
"Ah! why has heav'n prolong'd this hated breath,
Patient of horrours, to behold thy death?   555
O Hector! late thy parents' pride and joy,
The boast of nations! the defence of Troy!
To whom her safety and her fame she ow'd,
Her chief, her hero, and almost her god!
O fatal change! become in one sad day   560
A senseless corse! inanimated clay!"

   But not as yet the fatal news had spread
To fair Andromache, of Hector dead;

As yet no messenger had told his fate,
Nor ev'n his stay without the Scæan gate.   565
Far in the close recesses of the dome,
Pensive she plied the melancholy loom;
A growing work employ'd her secret hours,
Confus'dly gay with intermingled flow'rs.
Her fair-hair'd handmaids heat the brazen urn,   570
The bath preparing for her lord's return:
In vain : alas ! her lord returns no more !
Unbath'd he lies, and bleeds along the shore !
Now from the walls the clamours reach her ear,
And all her members shake with sudden fear;   575
Forth from her iv'ry hand the shuttle falls,
As thus, astonish'd, to her maids she calls:
    " Ah, follow me !" she cried; " what plaintive noise
Invades my ear ?   'Tis sure my mother's voice.
My falt'ring knees their trembling frame desert,   580
A pulse unusual flutters at my heart.
Some strange disaster, some reverse of fate
(Ye gods avert it !) threats the Trojan state.
Far be the omen which my thoughts suggest !
But much I fear my Hector's dauntless breast   585
Confronts Achilles; chas'd along the plain,
Shut from our walls ! I fear, I fear him slain !
Safe in the crowd he ever scorn'd to wait,

And sought for glory in the jaws of fate :
Perhaps that noble heat has cost his breath,   590
Now quench'd for ever in the arms of death."
   She spoke ; and, furious, with distracted pace,
Fears in her heart, and anguish in her face,
Flies thro' the dome (the maids her step pursue),
And mounts the walls, and sends around her view.   595
Too soon her eyes the killing object found,
The godlike Hector dragg'd along the ground.
A sudden darkness shades her swimming eyes :
She faints, she falls ; her breath, her colour flies.
Her hair's fair ornaments, the braids that bound,   600
The net that held them, and the wreath that crown'd,
The veil and diadem, flew far away
(The gift of Venus on her bridal day).
Around, a train of weeping sisters stands,
To raise her sinking with assistant hands.   605
Scarce from the verge of death recall'd, again
She faints, or but recovers to complain :
   " O wretched husband of a wretched wife !
Born with one fate, to one unhappy life !
For° sure one star its baneful beam display'd   610
On Priam's roof and Hippoplacia's shade.
From diff'rent parents, diff'rent climes, we came,
At diff'rent periods, yet our fate the same !

Why was my birth to great Eëtion ow'd,
And why was all that tender care bestow'd?   615
Would I had never been!—O thou, the ghost
Of my dead husband! miserably lost!
Thou to the dismal realms for ever gone!
And I abandon'd, desolate, alone!
An only child, once comfort of my pains,   620
Sad product now of hapless love, remains!
No more to smile upon his sire! no friend
To help him now! no father to defend!
For should he 'scape the sword, the common doom,
What wrongs attend him, and what griefs to come!   625
Ev'n from his own paternal roof expell'd,
Some stranger ploughs his patrimonial field.
The day that to the shades the father sends,
Robs the sad orphan of his father's friends:
He, wretched outcast of mankind! appears   630
For ever sad, for ever bath'd in tears;
Amongst the happy, unregarded he
Hangs on the robe or trembles at the knee;
While those his father's former bounty fed,
Nor reach the goblet, nor divide the bread: 635
The kindest but his present wants allay,
To leave him wretched the succeeding day.
Frugal compassion! Heedless, they who boast

Both parents still, nor feel what he has lost,
Shall cry, 'Begone!° thy father feasts not here': 640
The wretch obeys, retiring with a tear.
Thus wretched, thus retiring all in tears,
To my sad soul Astyanax appears!
Forc'd by repeated insults to return,
And to his widow'd mother vainly mourn, 645
He who, with tender delicacy bred,
With princes sported, and on dainties fed,
And, when still ev'ning gave him up to rest,
Sunk soft in down upon the nurse's breast, 649
Must — ah! what must he not? Whom Ilion calls
Astyanax, from her well-guarded walls,
Is now that name no more, unhappy boy!
Since now no more the father guards his Troy.
But thou, my Hector! liest expos'd in air,
Far from thy parents' and thy consort's care, 655
Whose hand in vain, directed by her love,
The martial scarf and robe of triumph wove.
Now to devouring flames be these a prey,
Useless to thee, from this accursed day!
Yet let the sacrifice at least be paid, 660
An honour to the living, not the dead!"
 So spake the mournful dame: her matrons hear,
Sigh back her sighs, and answer tear with tear.

BOOK XXIV

THE REDEMPTION OF THE BODY OF HECTOR

Now from the finish'd games° the Grecian band
Seek their black ships, and clear the crowded strand:
All stretch'd at ease the genial banquet share,
And pleasing slumbers quiet all their care.
Not so Achilles: he, to grief resign'd,   5
His friend's dear image present to his mind,
Takes his sad couch, more unobserv'd to weep,
Nor tastes the gifts of all-composing sleep;
Restless he roll'd around his weary bed,
And all his soul on his Patroclus fed: 10
The form so pleasing, and the heart so kind,
That youthful vigour, and that manly mind,
What toils they shar'd, what martial works they
        wrought,
What seas they measur'd, and what fields they fought;
All pass'd before him in rememb'rance dear,   15
Thought follows thought, and tear succeeds to tear.
And now supine, now prone, the hero lay,
Now shifts his side, impatient for the day;

Then starting up, disconsolate he goes
Wide° on the lonely beach to vent his woes.   20
There as the solitary mourner raves,
The ruddy morning rises o'er the waves:
Soon as it rose, his furious steeds he join'd;
The chariot flies, and Hector trails behind.
And thrice, Patroclus! round thy monument°   25
Was Hector dragg'd, then hurried to the tent.
There sleep at last o'ercomes the hero's eyes;
While foul in dust th' unhonour'd carcase lies,
But not deserted by the pitying skies.
For Phœbus watch'd it with superior care,   30
Preserv'd from gaping wounds, and tainting air;
And, ignominious as it swept the field,
Spread o'er the sacred corse his golden° shield.
All heav'n was mov'd, and Hermes° will'd to go
By stealth to snatch him from th' insulting foe: 35
But Neptune this, and Pallas this denies,
And th' unrelenting empress° of the skies:
E'er since that day implacable to Troy,
What time young Paris,° simple shepherd boy,
Won by destructive lust (reward obscene),   40
Their charms rejected for the Cyprian queen.
But when the tenth celestial morning broke,
To heav'n assembled, thus Apollo spoke:

"Unpitying pow'rs! how oft each holy fane
Has Hector ting'd with blood of victims slain!   45
And can ye still his cold remains pursue?
Still grudge his body to the Trojans' view?
Deny to consort, mother, son, and sire,
The last sad honours of a fun'ral fire?
Is then the dire Achilles all your care?   50
That iron heart, inflexibly severe;
A lion, not a man, who slaughters wide
In strength of rage and impotence of pride,
Who hastes to murder with a savage joy,
Invades around, and breathes but to destroy.   55
Shame° is not of his soul; nor understood
The greatest evil and the greatest good.
Still for one loss he rages unresign'd,
Repugnant to the lot of all mankind;
To lose a friend, a brother, or a son,   60
Heav'n dooms each mortal, and its will is done:
Awhile they sorrow, then dismiss their care;
Fate gives the wound, and man is born to bear.
But this insatiate the commission giv'n
By fate exceeds, and tempts the wrath of heav'n: 65
Lo how his rage dishonest drags along
Hector's dead earth, insensible of wrong!
Brave tho' he be, yet by no reason aw'd,

He violates the laws of man and God!"
"If equal honours by the partial skies   70
Are doom'd both heroes," Juno thus replies,
"If Thetis' son must no distinction know,
Then hear, ye gods! the patron of the bow.
But Hector only boasts a mortal claim,
His birth deriving from a mortal dame: 75
Achilles, of your own ethereal race,
Springs from a goddess, by a man's embrace
(A goddess by ourself to Peleus giv'n
A man divine, and chosen friend of heav'n):
To grace those nuptials, from the bright abode   80
Yourselves were present; where this minstrel-god
(Well-pleas'd to share the feast) amid the quire
Stood proud to hymn, and tune his youthful lyre."
    Then thus the Thund'rer checks th' imperial dame:
"Let not thy wrath the court of heav'n inflame;   85
Their merits nor their honours are the same.
But mine, and ev'ry god's peculiar grace
Hector deserves, of all the Trojan race:
Still on our shrines his grateful off'rings lay
(The only honours men to gods can pay),   90
Nor ever from our smoking altar ceas'd
The pure libation, and the holy feast.
Howe'er, by stealth to snatch the corse away,

We will not: Thetis guards it night and day.
But haste, and summon to our courts above   95
The azure° queen: let her persuasion move
Her furious son from Priam to receive
The proffer'd ransom, and the corse to leave."
　　He added not: and Iris° from the skies,
Swift as a whirlwind, on the message flies;   100
Meteorous the face of ocean sweeps,
Refulgent gliding o'er the sable deeps.
Between where Samos° wide his forests spreads,
And rocky Imbrus lifts its pointed heads,
Down plung'd the maid (the parted waves resound); 105
She plung'd, and instant shot the dark profound.
As, bearing death in the fallacious bait,
From° the bent angle sinks the leaden weight;
So pass'd the goddess thro' the closing wave,
Where Thetis sorrow'd in her secret cave: 110
There plac'd amidst her melancholy train
(The blue-hair'd° sisters of the sacred main)
Pensive she sat, revolving fates to come,
And wept her godlike son's approaching doom.
　　Then thus the goddess of the painted bow: 115
"Arise, O Thetis! from thy seats below;
'Tis Jove that calls." "And why," the dame replies,
"Calls Jove his Thetis to the hated skies?

Sad object as I am for heav'nly sight!
Ah! may my sorrows ever shun the light! 120
Howe'er, be heav'n's almighty sire obey'd."
She spake, and veil'd her head in sable shade,
Which, flowing long, her graceful person clad;
And forth she pac'd majestically sad.

Then through the world of waters they repair 125
(The way fair Iris led) to upper air.
The deeps dividing, o'er the coast they rise,
And touch with momentary flight the skies.
There in the light'ning's blaze the sire they found
And all the gods in shining synod round. 130
Thetis approach'd with anguish in her face
(Minerva rising gave the mourner place),
Ev'n Juno sought her sorrows to console,
And offer'd from her hand the nectar-bowl:
She tasted, and resign'd it: then began 135
The sacred sire of gods and mortal man:

"Thou com'st, fair Thetis, but with grief o'ercast,
Maternal sorrows, long, ah long to last!
Suffice, we know and we partake thy cares:
But yield to fate, and hear what Jove declares. 140
Nine days are past, since all the court above
In Hector's cause have mov'd the ear of Jove;
'Twas voted, Hermes from his godlike foe

By stealth should bear him, but we will'd not so :
We will, thy son himself the corse restore,   145
And to his conquest add this glory° more.
Then hie thee to him, and our mandate bear ;
Tell him he tempts the wrath of heav'n too far :
Nor let him more (our anger if he dread)
Vent his sad vengeance on the sacred dead :   150
But yield to ransom and the father's pray'r.
The mournful father Iris shall prepare,
With gifts to sue, and offer to his hands
Whate'er his honour asks or heart demands."

His word the silver-footed queen attends,   155
And from Olympus' snowy tops descends.
Arriv'd, she heard the voice of loud lament,
And echoing groans that shook the lofty tent.
His friends prepare the victim, and dispose
Repast unheeded, while he vents his woes.   160
The goddess seats her by her pensive son ;
She press'd his hand, and tender thus begun :

" How long, unhappy ! shall thy sorrows flow,
And thy heart waste with life-consuming woe,
Mindless of food, or love, whose pleasing reign   165
Soothes weary life, and softens human pain ?
Oh snatch the moments yet within thy pow'r ;
Not long to live, indulge the am'rous hour !

Lo! Jove himself (for Jove's command I bear)
Forbids to tempt the wrath of heav'n too far.   170
No longer then (his fury if thou dread)
Detain the relics of great Hector dead;
Nor vent on senseless earth thy vengeance vain,
But yield to ransom, and restore the slain."
    To whom Achilles: "Be the ransom giv'n,   175
And we submit, since such the will of heav'n."
    While thus they commun'd, from th' Olympian bow'rs
Jove orders Iris to the Trojan tow'rs:
"Haste, winged goddess, to the sacred town,
And urge her monarch to redeem his son;   180
Alone the Ilian ramparts let him leave,
And bear what stern Achilles may receive:
Alone, for so we will: no Trojan near,
Except, to place the dead with decent care,
Some aged herald, who, with gentle hand,   185
May the slow mules and fun'ral car command.
Nor let him death, nor let him danger dread,
Safe thro' the foe by our protection led:
Him Hermes to Achilles shall convey,
Guard of his life, and partner of his way.   190
Fierce as he is, Achilles' self shall spare
His age, nor touch one venerable hair:
Some thought there must be in a soul so brave,

Some sense of duty, some desire to save."
Then down her bow the winged Iris drives,   195
And swift at Priam's mournful court arrives:
Where the sad sons beside their father's throne
Sate bathed in tears, and answer'd groan with groan.
And all amidst them lay the hoary sire
(Sad scene of woe!), his face his wrapp'd attire   200
Conceal'd from sight; with frantic hands he spread
A show'r of ashes o'er his neck and head.
From room to room his pensive daughters roam:
Whose shrieks and clamours fill the vaulted dome;
Mindful of those who, late their pride and joy,   205
Lie pale and breathless round the fields of Troy!
Before the king Jove's messenger appears,
And thus in whispers greets his trembling ears:
"Fear not, O father! no ill news I bear;
From Jove I come, Jove makes thee still his care; 210
For Hector's sake these walls he bids thee leave,
And bear what stern Achilles may receive:
Alone, for so he wills: no Trojan near,
Except, to place the dead with decent care,
Some aged herald, who, with gentle hand,   215
May the slow mules and fun'ral car command.
Nor shalt thou death, nor shalt thou danger dread,
Safe thro' the foe by his protection led:

Thee Hermes to Pelides shall convey,
Guard of thy life, and partner of thy way.　　220
Fierce as he is, Achilles' self shall spare
Thy age, nor touch one venerable hair:
Some thought there must be in a soul so brave,
Some sense of duty, some desire to save."
　She spoke, and vanish'd.　Priam bids prepare　225
His gentle mules, and harness to the car;
There, for the gifts, a polish'd casket lay:
His pious sons the king's commands obey.
Then passed the monarch to his bridal-room,
Where cedar-beams the lofty roofs perfume,　　230
And where the treasures of his empire lay;
Then call'd his queen, and thus began to say:
　" Unhappy consort of a king distress'd!
Partake the troubles of thy husband's breast:
I saw descend the messenger of Jove,　　235
Who bids me try Achilles' mind to move,
Forsake these ramparts, and with gifts obtain
The corse of Hector, at yon navy slain.
Tell me thy thought: my heart impels to go
Thro' hostile camps, and bears me to the foe."　　240
　The hoary monarch thus: her piercing cries
Sad Hecuba renews, and then replies:
" Ah! whither wanders thy distemper'd mind;

H

And where the prudence now that aw'd mankind,
Thro' Phrygia once and foreign regions known?   245
Now all confus'd, distracted, overthrown!
Singly to pass thro' hosts of foes! to face
(O heart of steel!) the murd'rer of thy race!
To view that deathful eye, and wander o'er
Those hands, yet red with Hector's noble gore!   250
Alas! my lord! he knows not how to spare,
And what his mercy, thy slain sons declare;
So brave! so many fall'n! To calm his rage
Vain were thy dignity, and vain thy age.
No — pent in this sad palace, let us give   255
To grief the wretched days we have to live.
Still, still for Hector let our sorrows flow,
Born to his own and to his parents' woe!
Doom'd from the hour his luckless life begun,
To dogs, to vultures, and to Peleus' son!   260
Oh! in his dearest blood might I allay
My rage, and these barbarities repay!
For ah! could Hector merit thus, whose breath
Expir'd not meanly in unactive death?
He pour'd his latest blood in manly fight,   265
And fell a hero in his country's right."
    "Seek not to stay me, nor my soul affright
With words of omen, like a bird of night,"

Replied unmov'd the venerable man:
" 'Tis heav'n commands me, and you urge in vain. 270
Had any mortal voice th' injunction laid,
Nor augur, priest, nor seer had been obey'd.
A present goddess brought the high command:
I saw, I heard her, and the word shall stand.
I go, ye gods! obedient to your call: 275
If in yon camp your pow'rs have doom'd my fall,
Content: by the same hand let me expire!
Add to the slaughter'd son the wretched sire!
One cold embrace at least may be allow'd,
And my last tears flow mingled with his blood!" 280
  Forth from his open'd stores, this said, he drew
Twelve costly carpets of refulgent hue;
As many vests, as many mantles told,
And twelve fair veils, and garments stiff with gold;
Two tripods next, and twice two chargers° shine, 285
With ten pure talents from the richest mine;
And last a large, well-labour'd bowl had place
(The pledge of treaties once with friendly Thrace):
Seem'd all too mean the stores he could employ,
For one last look to buy him back to Troy! 290
  Lo! the sad father, frantic with his pain,
Around him furious drives his menial train:
In vain each slave with duteous care attends,

Each° office hurts him, and each face offends.
"What make ye here, officious crowds!" he cries ; 295
"Hence, nor obtrude your anguish on my eyes.
Have ye no griefs at home, to fix ye there?
Am I the only object of despair?
Am I become my people's common show,
Set up by Jove your spectacle of woe?   300
No, you must feel him too: yourselves must fall;
The same stern god to ruin gives you all:
Nor is great Hector lost by me alone;
Your sole defence, your guardian pow'r, is gone!
I see your blood the fields of Phrygia drown;   305
I see the ruins of your smoking town!
Oh send me, gods, ere that sad day shall come,
A willing ghost to Pluto's dreary dome!"
     He said, and feebly drives his friends away:
The sorrowing friends his frantic rage obey.   310
Next on his sons his erring° fury falls,
Polites, Paris, Agathon, he calls;
His threats Deïphobus and Dius hear,
Hippothoüs, Pammon, Helenus the seer,
And gen'rous Antiphon; for yet these nine   315
Surviv'd, sad relics of his num'rous line.
     "Inglorious sons of an unhappy sire!
Why did not all in Hector's cause expire?

Wretch that I am! my bravest offspring slain,
You, the disgrace of Priam's house, remain!   320
Mestor the brave, renown'd in ranks of war,
With Troilus,° dreadful on his rushing car,
And last great Hector, more than man divine,
For sure he seem'd not of terrestrial line!
All those relentless Mars untimely slew,   325
And left me these, a soft and servile crew,
Whose days the feast and wanton dance employ,
Gluttons and flatt'rers, the contempt of Troy!
Why teach ye not my rapid wheels to run,
And speed my journey to redeem my son?"   330
     The sons their father's wretched age revere,
Forgive his anger, and produce the car.
High on the seat the cabinet they bind:
The new-made car with solid beauty shin'd:
Box was the yoke, emboss'd with costly pains,   335
And hung with ringlets° to receive the reins:
Nine cubits long, the traces swept the ground;
These to the chariot's polish'd pole they bound,
Then fix'd a ring the running reins to guide,
And, close beneath, the gather'd ends were tied.   340
Next with the gifts (the price of Hector slain)
The sad attendants load the groaning wain:
Last to the yoke the well-match'd mules they bring

(The gift of Mysia to the Trojan king).
But the fair horses, long his darling care,   345
Himself receiv'd, and harness'd to his car:
Griev'd as he was, he not this task denied;
The hoary herald help'd him at his side.
While careful these the gentle coursers join'd,
Sad Hecuba approach'd with anxious mind;   350
A golden bowl, that foam'd with fragrant wine
(Libation destin'd to the pow'r divine),
Held in her right, before the steeds she stands,
And thus consigns it to the monarch's hands: 354
    "Take this, and pour to Jove; that, safe from harms,
His grace restore thee to our roof and arms.
Since, victor of thy fears, and slighting mine,
Heav'n or thy soul inspire this bold design,
Pray to that god° who, high on Ida's brow,
Surveys thy desolated realms below,   360
His winged° messenger to send from high,
And lead the way with heav'nly augury:
Let the strong sov'reign of the plumy race
Tow'r on the right of yon ethereal space.
That sign beheld, and strengthen'd from above,   365
Boldly pursue the journey mark'd by Jove;
But if the god his augury denies,
Suppress thy impulse, nor reject advice."

" 'Tis just," said Priam, " to the sire above
To raise our hands ; for who so good as Jove ? "   370
   He spoke, and bade th' attendant handmaid bring
The purest water of the living spring
(Her ready hands the ewer and bason held);
Then took the golden cup his queen had fill'd ;
On the mid° pavement pours the rosy wine,   375
Uplifts his eyes, and calls the pow'r divine:
   " O first and greatest! heav'n's imperial lord!
On lofty Ida's holy hill ador'd!
To stern Achilles now direct my ways,
And teach him mercy when a father prays.   380
If such thy will, dispatch from yonder sky
Thy sacred bird, celestial augury !
Let the strong sov'reign of the plumy race
Tow'r on the right of yon ethereal space:
So shall thy suppliant, strengthen'd from above,   385
Fearless pursue the journey mark'd by Jove."
   Jove heard his pray'r, and from the throne on high
Dispatch'd his bird, celestial augury !
The swift-wing'd chaser of the feather'd game,
And known to gods by Percnos'° lofty name.   390
Wide as appears some palace-gate display'd,
So broad his pinions stretch'd their ample shade,
As, stooping dexter° with resounding wings,

Th' imperial bird descends in airy rings.
A dawn of joy in ev'ry face appears;   395
The mourning matron dries her tim'rous tears.
Swift on his car th' impatient monarch sprung;
The brazen portal in his passage rung.
The mules preceding draw the loaded wain,
Charg'd with the gifts; Idæus holds the rein: 400
The king himself his gentle steeds controls,
And thro' surrounding friends the chariot rolls:
On his slow wheels the following people wait,
Mourn at each step, and give him up to fate;
With hands uplifted, eye him as he pass'd,   405
And gaze upon him as they gaz'd their last.

Now forward fares the father on his way,
Thro' the lone fields, and back to Ilion they.
Great Jove beheld him as he cross'd the plain,
And felt the woes of miserable man.   410
Then thus to Hermes : "Thou, whose constant cares
Still succour mortals, and attend their pray'rs!
Behold an object to thy charge consign'd;
If ever pity touch'd thee for mankind,
Go, guard the sire; th' observing foe prevent,   415
And safe conduct him to Achilles' tent."

The god obeys, his golden pinions binds,
And mounts incumbent° on the wings of winds,

That high thro' fields of air his flight sustain,
O'er the wide earth, and o'er the boundless main : 420
Then grasps the wand that causes sleep to fly,
Or in soft slumbers seals the wakeful eye :
Thus arm'd, swift Hermes steers his airy way,
And stoops on Hellespont's resounding sea.
A beauteous youth, majestic and divine, 425
He seem'd ; fair offspring of some princely line!
Now twilight veil'd the glaring face of day,
And clad the dusky fields in sober grey ;
What time the herald and the hoary king,
Their chariot stopping at the silver° spring, 430
That circling Ilus'° ancient marble flows,
Allow'd their mules and steeds a short repose.
Thro' the dim shade the herald first espies
A man's approach, and thus to Priam cries :
" I mark some foe's advance : O king! beware ; 435
This hard adventure claims thy utmost care ;
For much I fear destruction hovers nigh :
Our state asks counsel.   Is it best to fly ?
Or, old and helpless, at his feet to fall
(Two wretched suppliants), and for mercy call ? " 440
    Th' afflicted monarch shiver'd with despair ;
Pale grew his face, and upright stood his hair ;
Sunk was his heart ; his colour went and came ;

A sudden trembling shook his aged frame :
When Hermes, greeting, touch'd his royal hand, 445
And, gentle, thus accosts with kind demand :
  " Say whither, father ! when each mortal sight
Is seal'd in sleep, thou wander'st thro' the night.
Why roam thy mules and steeds the plains along,
Thro' Grecian foes, so num'rous and so strong ? 450
What couldst thou hope, should these thy treasures
     view,
These, who with endless hate thy race pursue?
For what defence, alas ! couldst thou provide,
Thyself not young, a weak old man thy guide ?
Yet suffer not thy soul to sink with dread ; 455
From me no harm shall touch thy rev'rend head :
From Greece I'll guard thee too ; for in those lines°
The living image of my father shines."
  " Thy words, that speak benevolence of mind,
Are true, my son ! " the godlike sire rejoin'd : 460
" Great are my hazards ; but the gods survey
My steps, and send thee guardian of my way.
Hail ! and be blest ! for scarce of mortal kind
Appear thy form, thy feature, and thy mind."
  " Nor true are all thy words, nor erring wide," 465
The sacred messenger of heav'n replied :
" But say, convey'st thou thro' the lonely plains

What yet most precious of thy store remains,
To lodge in safety with some friendly hand,
Prepar'd perchance to leave thy native land?   470
Or fly'st thou now? What hopes can Troy retain,
Thy matchless son, her guard and glory, slain?"
    The king, alarm'd: "Say what, and whence thou art,
Who search the sorrows of a parent's heart,
And know so well how godlike Hector died."   475
Thus Priam spoke, and Hermes thus replied:
    "You tempt me, father, and with pity touch:
On this sad subject you enquire too much.
Oft have these eyes the godlike Hector view'd
In glorious fight, with Grecian blood embru'd: 480
I saw him when, like Jove, his flames he toss'd
On thousand ships, and wither'd half a host:
I saw, but help'd not; stern Achilles' ire
Forbade assistance, and enjoy'd the fire.
For him I serve, of Myrmidonian race;   485
One ship convey'd us from our native place;
Polyctor is my sire, an honour'd name,
Old, like thyself, and not unknown to fame;
Of sev'n his sons, by whom the lot was cast
To serve our prince, it fell on me the last.   490
To watch this quarter my adventure falls;
For with the morn the Greeks attack your walls;

Sleepless they sit, impatient to engage,
And scarce their rulers check their martial rage."
  "If then thou art of stern Pelides' train "   495
(The mournful monarch thus rejoin'd again),
"Ah, tell me truly, where, oh! where are laid
My son's dear relics? what befalls him dead?
Have dogs dismember'd on the naked plains,
Or yet unmangled rest his cold remains?"   500
  "O favour'd of the skies!" thus answer'd then
The pow'r that mediates between gods and men,
"Nor dogs nor vultures have thy Hector rent,
But whole he lies, neglected in the tent:
This the twelfth ev'ning since he rested there,   505
Untouch'd by worms, untainted by the air.
Still as Aurora's ruddy beam is spread,
Round his friend's tomb Achilles drags the dead;
Yet undisfigur'd, or in limb or face,
All fresh he lies, with ev'ry living grace,   510
Majestical in death! No stains are found
O'er all the corse, and clos'd is ev'ry wound;
Tho' many a wound they gave. Some heav'nly care,
Some hand divine, preserves him ever fair:
Or all the host of heav'n, to whom he led   515
A life so grateful, still regard him dead."
  Thus spoke to Priam the celestial guide,

And joyful thus the royal sire replied :
" Bless'd is the man who pays the gods above
The constant tribute of respect and love ! 520
Those who inhabit the Olympian bow'r
My son forgot not, in exalted pow'r;
And heav'n, that ev'ry virtue bears in mind,
Ev'n to the ashes of the just is kind.
But thou, O gen'rous youth! this goblet take, 525
A pledge of gratitude for Hector's sake ;
And while the fav'ring gods our steps survey,
Safe to Pelides' tent conduct my way."
 To whom the latent god : " O king, forbear
To tempt my youth, for apt is youth to err : 530
But can I, absent from my prince's sight,
Take gifts in secret, that must shun the light ?
What from our master's int'rest thus we draw
Is but a licens'd theft that 'scapes the law.
Respecting him, my soul abjures th' offence ; 535
And, as the crime, I dread the consequence.
Thee, far as Argos, pleas'd I could convey ;
Guard of thy life, and partner of thy way :
On thee attend, thy safety to maintain,
O'er pathless forests, or the roaring main." 540
 He said, then took the chariot at a bound,
And snatch'd the reins, and whirl'd the lash around :

Before th' inspiring god that urg'd them on
The coursers fly, with spirit not their own.
And now they reach'd the naval walls, and found   545
The guards repasting, while the bowls go round:
On these the virtue of his wand he tries,
And pours deep slumber on their watchful eyes:
Then heav'd the massy gates, remov'd the bars,
And o'er the trenches led the rolling cars.   550
Unseen, thro' all the hostile camp they went,
And now approach'd Pelides' lofty tent.°
Of fir the roof was rais'd, and cover'd o'er
With reeds collected from the marshy shore;
And, fenc'd with palisades, a hall of state   555
(The work of soldiers), where the hero sate.
Large was the door, whose well-compacted strength
A solid pine-tree barr'd of wond'rous length;
Scarce three strong Greeks could lift its mighty weight,
But great Achilles singly clos'd the gate.   560
This Hermes (such the pow'r of gods) set wide;
Then swift alighted the celestial guide,
• And thus, reveal'd: "Hear, prince! and understand
Thou ow'st thy guidance to no mortal hand;
Hermes I am, descended from above,   565
The king of arts, the messenger of Jove.
Farewell: to shun Achilles' sight I fly;

Uncommon are such favours of the sky,
Nor stand confess'd to frail mortality.
Now fearless enter, and prefer thy pray'rs;   570
Adjure him by his father's silver hairs,
His son,° his mother! urge him to bestow
Whatever pity that stern heart can know."
    Thus having said, he vanish'd from his eyes,
And in a moment shot into the skies: 575
The king, confirm'd from heav'n, alighted there,
And left his aged herald on the car.
With solemn pace thro' various rooms he went,
And found Achilles in his inner tent:
There sate the hero; Alcimus the brave,   580
And great Automedon, attendance gave;
These serv'd his person at the royal feast;
Around, at awful distance, stood the rest.
    Unseen by these, the king his entry made;
And, prostrate now before Achilles laid,   585
Sudden° (a venerable sight!) appears;
Embrac'd his knees, and bath'd his hands in tears;
Those direful hands his kisses press'd, embru'd
Ev'n with the best, the dearest of his blood!
    As when a wretch (who, conscious of his crime,   590
Pursu'd for murder flies his native clime)
Just gains some frontier, breathless, pale, amaz'd!

All gaze, all wonder: thus Achilles gaz'd:
Thus stood th' attendants stupid with surprise:
All mute, yet seem'd to question with their eyes: 595
Each look'd on other, none the silence broke,
Till thus at last the kingly suppliant spoke:
  "Ah° think, thou favour'd of the pow'rs divine!
Think of thy father's age, and pity mine!
In me, that father's rev'rend image trace,   600
Those silver hairs, that venerable face;
His trembling limbs, his helpless person, see!
In all my equal, but in misery!
Yet now, perhaps, some turn of human fate
Expels him helpless from his peaceful state;   605
Think, from some pow'rful foe thou see'st him fly,
And beg protection with a feeble cry.
Yet still one comfort in his soul may rise;
He hears his son still lives to glad his eyes;
And, hearing, still may hope a better day   610
May send him thee, to chase that foe away.
No comfort to my griefs, no hopes remain,
The best, the bravest, of my sons are slain!
Yet what a race! ere Greece to Ilion came,
The pledge of many a lov'd and loving dame!   615
Nineteen one mother bore — dead, all are dead!
How oft, alas! has wretched Priam bled!

Still one was left, their loss to recompense;
His father's hope, his country's last defence.
Him too thy rage has slain! beneath thy steel, 620
Unhappy, in his country's cause, he fell!
For him thro' hostile camps I bent my way,
For him thus prostrate at thy feet I lay;
Large gifts, proportion'd to thy wrath, I bear:
Oh, hear the wretched, and the gods revere! 625
Think of thy father, and this face behold!
See him in me, as helpless and as old;
Tho' not so wretched: there he yields to me,
The first of men in sov'reign misery:
Thus forc'd to kneel, thus grov'ling to embrace 630
The scourge and ruin of my realm and race:
Suppliant my children's murd'rer to implore,
And kiss those hands yet reeking with their gore!"
These words soft pity in the chief inspire,
Touch'd with the dear rememb'rance of his sire. 635
Then with his hand (as prostrate still he lay)
The old man's cheek he gently turn'd away.
Now each by turns indulg'd the gush of woe;
And now the mingled tides together flow:
This low on earth, that gently bending o'er, 640
A father one, and one a son deplore:
But great Achilles diff'rent passions rend,

i

And now his sire he mourns, and now his friend.
Th' infectious softness thro' the heroes ran;
One universal solemn show'r began;   645
They bore as heroes, but they felt as man.
　　Satiate at length with unavailing woes,
From the high throne divine Achilles rose;
The rev'rend monarch by the hand he rais'd;
On his white beard and form majestic gaz'd,   650
Not unrelenting: then serene began
With words to soothe the miserable man:
　　"Alas! what weight of anguish hast thou known,
Unhappy prince! thus guardless and alone
To pass thro' foes, and thus undaunted face   655
The man whose fury has destroy'd thy race!
Heav'n sure has arm'd thee with a heart of steel,
A strength proportion'd to the woes you feel.
Rise then: let reason mitigate our care:
To mourn avails not: man is born to bear.   660
Such is, alas! the gods' severe decree;
They, only they are blest, and only free.
Two urns by Jove's high throne have ever stood,
The source of evil one, and one of good;
From thence the cup of mortal man he fills,   665
Blessings to these, to those distributes ills;
To most he mingles both: the wretch decreed

To taste the bad unmix'd, is curs'd indeed:
Pursu'd by wrongs, by meagre famine driv'n,
He wanders, outcast both of earth and heav'n. 670
The happiest taste not happiness sincere,
But find the cordial draught is dash'd with care.
Who more than Peleus shone in wealth and pow'r?
What stars concurring bless'd his natal hour!
A realm, a goddess, to his wishes giv'n, 675
Grac'd by the gods with all the gifts of heav'n!
One evil, yet, o'ertakes his latest day;
No race succeeding to imperial sway:
An only son! and he (alas!) ordain'd
To fall untimely in a foreign land! 680
See him, in Troy, the pious care decline
Of his weak age, to live the curse of thine!
Thou too, old man, hast happier days beheld;
In riches once, in children once excell'd;
Extended Phrygia own'd thy ample reign, 685
And all fair Lesbos' blissful seats contain,
And all wide Hellespont's unmeasur'd main.
But since the god his hand has pleas'd to turn,
And fill thy measure from his bitter urn,
What sees the sun but hapless heroes' falls? 690
War and the blood of men surround thy walls!
What must be, must be. Bear thy lot, nor shed

These unavailing sorrows o'er the dead;
Thou canst not call him from the Stygian shore,
But thou, alas! mayst live to suffer more!"　　　　695
　　To whom the king: "O favour'd of the skies!
Here let me grow to earth! since Hector lies
On the bare beach, depriv'd of obsequies.
Oh, give me Hector! to my eyes restore
His corse, and take the gifts: I ask no more!　　　　700
Thou, as thou mayst, these boundless stores enjoy;
Safe mayst thou sail, and turn thy wrath from Troy;
So shall thy pity and forbearance give
A weak old man to see the light and live!"
　　"Move me no more," Achilles thus replies,　　　　705
While kindling anger sparkled in his eyes,
"Nor seek by tears my steady soul to bend.
To yield thy Hector I myself intend:
For know, from Jove my goddess-mother came
(Old Ocean's daughter, silver-footed dame);　　　　710
Nor com'st thou but by heav'n; nor com'st alone;
Some god impels with courage not thy own:
No human hand the weighty gates unbarr'd,
Nor could the boldest of our youth have dar'd
To pass our out-works, or elude the guard.　　　　715
Cease; lest, neglectful of high Jove's command,
I show thee, king! thou tread'st on hostile land;

Release my knees, thy suppliant arts give o'er,
And shake the purpose of my soul no more."
  The sire obey'd him, trembling and o'eraw'd.   720
Achilles, like a lion, rush'd abroad;
Automedon and Alcimus attend,
Whom most he honour'd since he lost his friend;
These to unyoke the mules and horses went,
And led the hoary herald to the tent: 725
Next, heap'd on high, the num'rous presents bear
(Great Hector's ransom) from the polish'd car.
Two splendid mantles, and a carpet spread,
They leave, to cover and inwrap the dead:
Then call the handmaids, with assistant toil   730
To wash the body, and anoint with oil,
Apart from Priam; lest th' unhappy sire,
Provok'd to passion, once more rouse to ire
The stern Pelides; and nor sacred age
Nor Jove's command should check the rising rage.   735
This done, the garments o'er the corse they spread;
Achilles lifts it to the fun'ral bed:
Then, while the body on the car they laid,
He groans, and calls on lov'd Patroclus' shade:
  "If, in that gloom which never light must know,   740
The deeds of mortals touch the ghosts below;
O friend! forgive me, that I thus fulfil

(Restoring Hector) heaven's unquestion'd will.
The gifts the father gave, be ever thine,
To grace thy manes,° and adorn thy shrine."   745
   He said, and, ent'ring, took his seat of state,
Where full before him rev'rend Priam sate:
To whom, compos'd, the godlike chief begun:
"Lo! to thy pray'r restor'd, thy breathless son;
Extended on the fun'ral couch he lies;   750
And, soon as morning paints the eastern skies,
The sight is granted to thy longing eyes.
But now the peaceful hours of sacred night
Demand refection, and to rest invite:
Nor thou, O father! thus consum'd with woe,   755
The common cares that nourish life forego.
Not thus did Niobe,° of form divine,
A parent once, whose sorrows equall'd thine:
Six youthful sons, as many blooming maids,
In one sad day beheld the Stygian shades: 760
Those by Apollo's silver bow were slain,
These Cynthia's° arrows stretch'd upon the plain.
So was her pride chastis'd by wrath divine,
Who match'd her own with bright Latona's line;
But two the goddess, twelve the queen enjoy'd;   765
Those boasted twelve th' avenging two destroy'd.
Steep'd in their blood, and in the dust outspread,

Nine days neglected lay expos'd the dead;
None by to weep them, to inhume° them none
(For Jove had turn'd the nation all to stone);   770
The gods themselves, at length, relenting, gave
Th' unhappy race the honours of a grave.
Herself° a rock (for such was heav'n's high will)
Thro' deserts wild now pours a weeping rill;
Where round the bed whence Acheloüs springs,   775
The wat'ry fairies dance in mazy rings:
There, high on Sipylus's shady brow,
She stands, her own sad monument of woe;
The rock for ever lasts, the tears for ever flow.
Such griefs, O king! have other parents known: 780
Remember theirs, and mitigate thy own.
The care of heav'n thy Hector has appear'd;
Nor shall he lie unwept and uninterr'd;
Soon may thy aged cheeks in tears be drown'd,
And all the eyes of Ilion stream around."   785

   He said, and, rising, chose the victim ewe
With silver fleece, which his attendants slew.
The limbs they sever from the reeking hide,
With skill prepare them, and in parts divide:
Each on the coals the sep'rate morsels lays,   790
And hasty snatches from the rising blaze.
With bread the glitt'ring canisters they load,

Which round the board Automedon bestow'd:
The chief himself to each his portion plac'd,
And each indulging shar'd in sweet repast. 795
When now the rage of hunger was repress'd,
The wond'ring hero eyes his royal guest;
No less the royal guest the hero eyes,
His godlike aspect and majestic size;
Here youthful grace and noble fire engage, 800
And there the mild benevolence of age.
Thus gazing long, the silence neither broke
(A solemn scene!); at length the father spoke:
"Permit me now, belov'd of Jove, to steep
My careful temples in the dew of sleep: 805
For since the day that number'd with the dead
My hapless son, the dust has been my bed;
Soft sleep a stranger to my weeping eyes,
My only food, my sorrows and my sighs!
Till now, encourag'd by the grace you give, 810
I share thy banquet, and consent to live."
    With that, Achilles bade prepare the bed,
With purple soft and shaggy carpets spread;
Forth, by the flaming lights, they bend their way,
And place the couches, and the cov'rings lay. 815
Then he: "Now, father, sleep, but sleep not here,
Consult thy safety, and forgive my fear,

Lest any Argive (at this hour awake,
To ask our counsel or our orders take),
Approaching sudden to our open tent,   820
Perchance behold thee, and our grace prevent.
Should such report thy honour'd person here,
The king of men the ransom might defer.
But say with speed, if aught of thy desire
Remains unask'd, what time the rites require 825
T' inter thy Hector. For, so long we stay
Our slaught'ring arm, and bid the hosts obey."
 "If then thy will permit," the monarch said,
"To finish all due honours to the dead,
This, of thy grace, accord: to thee are known 830
The fears of Ilion, clos'd within her town;
And at what distance from our walls aspire
The hills of Ide, and forests for the fire.
Nine days to vent our sorrows I request,
The tenth shall see the fun'ral and the feast; 835
The next, to raise his monument be giv'n;
The twelfth we war, if war be doom'd by heav'n!"
 "This thy request," replied the chief, "enjoy:
Till then our arms suspend the fall of Troy."
Then gave his hand at parting, to prevent 840
The old man's fears, and turn'd within the tent;
Where fair Briseïs, bright in blooming charms,

Expects her hero with desiring arms.
But in the porch the king and herald rest,
Sad dreams of care yet wand'ring in their breast.   845
   Now gods and men the gifts of sleep partake;
Industrious Hermes only was awake,
The king's return revolving in his mind,
To pass the ramparts and the watch to blind.
The pow'r descending hover'd o'er his head,   850
And, "Sleep'st thou, father?" (thus the vision said)
"Now dost thou sleep, when Hector is restor'd?
Nor fear the Grecian foes or Grecian lord?
Thy presence here should stern Atrides see,
Thy still-surviving sons may sue for thee;   855
May offer all thy treasures yet contain,
To spare thy age; and offer all in vain."
   Wak'd with the word, the trembling sire arose,
And rais'd his friend: the god before him goes:
He joins the mules, directs them with his hand,   860
And moves in silence thro' the hostile land.
When now to Xanthus' yellow stream they drove
(Xanthus, immortal progeny of Jove),
The winged deity forsook their view,
And in a moment to Olympus flew.   865
   Now shed Aurora round her saffron ray,
Sprung thro' the gates of light, and gave the day.

Charg'd with their mournful load, to Ilion go
The sage and king, majestically slow.
Cassandra first beholds, from Ilion's spire,   870
The sad procession of her hoary sire;
Then, as the pensive pomp advanc'd more near
(Her breathless brother stretch'd upon the bier),
A show'r of tears o'erflows her beauteous eyes,
Alarming thus all Ilion with her cries: 875
  "Turn here your steps, and here your eyes employ,
Ye wretched daughters and ye sons of Troy!
If e'er ye rush'd in crowds, with vast delight,
To hail your hero glorious from the fight;
Now meet him dead, and let your sorrows flow!   880
Your common triumph and your common woe."
  In thronging crowds they issue to the plains,
Nor man nor woman in the walls remains:
In ev'ry face the self-same grief is shown,
And Troy sends forth one universal groan.   885
At Scæa's gates, they meet the mourning wain,
Hang on the wheels, and grovel round the slain.
The wife and mother, frantic with despair,
Kiss his pale cheek, and rend their scatter'd hair;
Thus wildly wailing, at the gates they lay;   890
And there had sigh'd and sorrow'd out the day;
But godlike Priam from the chariot rose;

"Forbear," he cried, "this violence of woes;
First to the palace let the car proceed,
Then pour your boundless sorrows o'er the dead."   895
    The waves of people at his word divide;
Slow rolls the chariot thro' the following tide:
Ev'n to the palace the sad pomp they wait:
They weep, and place him on the bed of state.
A melancholy choir attend around,   900
With plaintive sighs and music's solemn sound:
Alternately they sing, alternate flow
Th' obedient tears, melodious in their woe;
While deeper sorrows groan from each full heart,
And nature speaks at ev'ry pause of art.   905
    First° to the corse the weeping consort flew;
Around his neck her milk-white arms she threw:
And, "O my Hector! O my lord!" she cries,
"Snatch'd in thy bloom from these desiring eyes!
Thou to the dismal realms for ever gone!   910
And I abandon'd, desolate, alone!
An only son, once comfort of our pains,
Sad product now of hapless love, remains!
Never to manly age that son shall rise,
Or with increasing graces glad my eyes;   915
For Ilion now (her great defender slain)
Shall sink, a smoking ruin, on the plain.

Who now protects her wives with guardian care?
Who saves her infants from the rage of war?
Now hostile fleets must waft those infants o'er 920
(Those wives must wait 'em) to a foreign shore!
Thou too, my son! to barb'rous climes shalt go,
The sad companion of thy mother's woe;
Driv'n hence a slave before the victor's sword,
Condemn'd to toil for some inhuman lord: 925
Or else some Greek, whose father press'd the plain,
Or son, or brother, by great Hector slain,
In Hector's blood his vengeance shall enjoy,
And hurl thee headlong from the tow'rs of Troy.
For thy stern father never spar'd a foe: 930
Thence all these tears, and all this scene of woe!
Thence many evils his sad parents bore,
His parents many, but his consort more.
Why° gav'st thou not to me thy dying hand?
And why receiv'd not I thy last command? 935
Some word thou wouldst have spoke, which, sadly dear,
My soul might keep, or utter with a tear;
Which never, never could be lost in air,
Fix'd in my heart, and oft repeated there!"
   Thus to her weeping maids she makes her moan: 940
Her weeping handmaids echo groan for groan.
   The mournful mother next sustains her part:

"O thou, the best, the dearest of my heart!
Of all my race thou most by heav'n approv'd,
And by th' immortals ev'n in death belov'd!   945
While all my other sons in barb'rous bands
Achilles bound, and sold to foreign lands,
This felt no chains, but went, a glorious ghost,
Free and a hero, to the Stygian coast.
Sentenc'd, 'tis true, by his inhuman doom,   950
Thy noble corse was dragg'd around the tomb
(The tomb of him thy warlike arm had slain);
Ungen'rous insult, impotent and vain!
Yet glow'st thou fresh with ev'ry living grace,
No mark of pain, or violence of face;   955
Rosy and fair! as Phœbus' silver bow
Dismiss'd thee gently to the shades below!"
    Thus spoke the dame, and melted into tears.
Sad Helen next in pomp of grief appears:
Fast from the shining sluices of her eyes   960
Fall the round crystal drops, while thus she cries:
"Ah,° dearest friend! in whom the gods had join'd
The mildest manners with the bravest mind!
Now twice ten years (unhappy years) are o'er
Since Paris brought me to the Trojan shore   965
(Oh had I perish'd, ere that form divine
Seduc'd this soft, this easy heart of mine!);

Yet was it ne'er my fate from thee to find
A deed ungentle, or a word unkind :
When others curs'd the auth'ress of their woe,   970
Thy pity check'd my sorrows in their flow :
If some proud brother ey'd me with disdain,
Or scornful sister with her sweeping train,
Thy gentle accents soften'd all my pain.
For thee I mourn ; and mourn myself in thee,   975
The wretched source of all this misery !
The fate I caus'd, for ever I bemoan ;
Sad Helen has no friend, now thou art gone !
Thro' Troy's wide streets abandon'd shall I roam,
In Troy deserted, as abhorr'd at home ! "   980
   So spoke the fair, with sorrow-streaming eye :
Distressful beauty melts each stander-by ;
On all around th' infectious sorrow grows ;
But Priam check'd the torrent as it rose :
"Perform, ye Trojans ! what the rites require,   985
And fell the forests for a fun'ral pyre !
Twelve days nor foes nor secret ambush dread ;
Achilles grants these honours to the dead."
   He spoke ; and at his word the Trojan train
Their mules and oxen harness to the wain,   990
Pour thro' the gates, and, fell'd from Ida's crown,
Roll back the gather'd forests to the town.

These toils continue nine succeeding days,
And high in air a sylvan structure raise.
But when the tenth fair morn began to shine,   995
Forth to the pile was borne the man divine,
And plac'd aloft: while all, with streaming eyes,
Beheld the flames and rolling smokes arise.
  Soon as Aurora, daughter of the dawn,
With rosy lustre streak'd the dewy lawn,   1000
Again the mournful crowds surround the pyre,
And quench with wine the yet-remaining fire.
The snowy bones his friends and brothers place
(With tears collected) in a golden vase;
The golden vase in purple palls they roll'd,   1005
Of softest texture and inwrought with gold.
Last, o'er the urn the sacred earth they spread,
And rais'd the tomb, memorial of the dead
(Strong guards and spies, till all the rites were done,
Watch'd from the rising to the setting sun).   1010
All Troy then moves to Priam's court again,
A solemn, silent, melancholy train:
Assembled there, from pious toil they rest,
And sadly shar'd the last sepulchral feast.
  Such° honours Ilion to her hero paid,   1015
And peaceful slept the mighty Hector's shade.

NOTES

Iliad. Poem about Ilion, or Troy. A form of title often given to an epic poem. Cf. *Æneid, Rolliad, Columbiad, Dunciad,* etc.

1. **Achilles' wrath.** The anger of Achilles is proposed by the poet himself as the subject of his poem. Μῆνιν, meaning *wrath,* is the first word of the poem. The poet begins with the wrath of Achilles, because it gave a decided impulse to the events of the war and hastened the catastrophe. It brought upon the Greeks a train of disasters, ending with the death of Patroclus, the beloved friend of Achilles, which drew him forth from his retirement, to exact a bloody vengeance from Hector and the Trojans. The purpose of Jove was to bring about the destruction of Troy by the fall of Hector, etc. And the will of Jove was accomplishing from the time when Atrides, King of Men, and the divine Achilles parted, having quarrelled. (Felton.)

2. **goddess :** the muse. The poet, inspired by the gods, invokes the aid of the Epic Muse. The "nine muses" are not mentioned by Homer, although the muses appear in the plural in several places. According to Hesiod they are the daughters

K 129

of Zeus and Memory, "a transparent allegory of the inspiration
needed by a poet who does not write, but has to compose and
recite his song by heart." (Leaf.)

3. **Pluto.** The god of the underworld, the abode of the dead.

4. **reign.** The territory of a sovereign, realm.

5. **unburied.** The souls of the unburied dead were supposed
to wander upon the banks of the Styx.

> "Behold a ghastly band,
>   Each a torch in his hand!
>   Those are Grecian ghosts, that in battle
>   were slain,
>   And unburied remain
>   Inglorious on the plain."
> — *Alexander's Feast.*

7. **Atrides.** Agamemnon, son of Atreus; so Achilles is
called Pelides, son of Peleus; and Diomedes is called Tydides,
son of Tydeus.

8. Observe the change of metre in the introduction of this
Alexandrine.

11. **Latona's son.** Apollo, the tutelary deity of the Dorians.
The Dorians had not at this time become the predominant race
in Greece. Throughout the *Iliad* Apollo acts splendidly and
effectively, but always against the Greeks, from mere partiality
to Hector.

13. **king of men.** Agamemnon.

13. **rev'rend priest:** Chryses.

20. **the sceptre and the laurel crown.** The golden sceptre
indicated that Chryses was the priest of Apollo. The laurel

crown is Pope's substitution for "the woollen fillet" of Homer,
which, wound round a staff, was the mark of the suppliant. "It
is here perhaps the same fillet which the priest usually wears on
his head in sign of his divine office. Or possibly it may even
be a fillet from the head of the god himself, and thus have still
higher sanctity." (Leaf.)

22. **brother-kings.** Agamemnon and Menelaus.

23–30. Notice the art of this speech. Chryses comprehen-
sively addresses the army of the Greeks as made up of troops
partly from the kingdoms and partly from democracies. As
priest of Apollo he prays that they may obtain the blessings
they desire — the conquest of Troy and a safe return. He then
names his petition, offers ransom, and bids them fear the wrath
of Apollo if they refuse his prayer. "Thus he endeavors to
work by the art of a general application, by religion, by interest,
and the insinuation of danger."

28. **Chryseïs.** Daughter of Chryses.

30. **Phœbus.** The *bright.* Homer usually speaks of Phœbus
Apollo, but the names are also sometimes separated.

32. **the fair.** A conventional poetic expression common in
the eighteenth century.

45. **Argos.** Not the town, but the Peloponnesus. See VI., 189.

50. Chryses does not reply to the insults of Agamemnon,
but walks silently and sadly by the sea. Pope says: "The
melancholy flowing of the verse admirably expresses the condition of the mournful and deserted father."

53. Smintheus. Literally Mouse-god. Apollo was worshipped under this title in the Troad, as at Smyrna as the Locust-god. The old explanation of the name was that Apollo gained it by ridding the land of a plague of field-mice. Mr. Andrew Lang sees in the title an indication of the existence of an old tribal totem or family ancestor. The mouse in Oriental countries often personified plague and disease. Herodotus ascribes the destruction of the army of Sennacherib to an army of field-mice, which came in the night and gnawed the Assyrian bowstrings. In 1 Sam. vi. 4 golden mice are offered by the Philistines as a propitiation when visited by the plague. It may therefore be that the god has this name only in virtue of his function of bringing and removing pestilence, of which this book of the *Iliad* is the best instance. In that case the appeal of Chryses gives him this title with peculiar appropriateness. (Leaf.)

54–56. Cilla and **Chrysa** are towns in the south of the Troad, on the gulf of Adramyttium ; Tenedos, an island in the bay of Troas. Apollo had temples at these places.

60. Apollo was believed to resent ill usage of his priests and that, too, in the way here represented, viz., by sending plagues.

61–68. The description of Apollo descending in wrath is celebrated ; the sound of the verse corresponds to the sense. Pope has sought by the use of onomatopœia and alliteration to imitate the twang of the silver bow and the sound of the flight of the arrows. Cowper, in his attempt to reproduce the effect of the original, produced a singular line, for which he felt it necessary to apologize —

"Clang'd the cord
Dread-sounding, bounding on the silver bow."

66. **around.** Some editions read *about.* Milton was the first to use *around* in the modern sense. Shakespeare uses *about;* Pope prefers *around.*

74. **Juno** (Hera). The wife of Jupiter ; she sided with the Greeks. Coleridge believed that Juno expressed the spirit of conservatism. She is persistent, obstinate, acts from no idea, but often uses a superficial reasoning, and refers to Fate, with which she upbraids Jupiter.

Thetis, daughter of Nereus and wife of Peleus, was the mother of Achilles.

81-82. **spare — war.** Notice the muffled rhyme.

88. Hecatomb means properly, as its etymology indicates, a sacrifice of a hundred oxen ; it is frequently used, however, to mean a sacrifice of any sort.

86. "It will be noticed that the soothsaying of the Homeric army is very far removed from the elaborate system with which we are acquainted in later Greece and Rome. The words of Achilles show that it was not confined to the priestly office, though the priest, from the relations which he had with his god, was likely to be specially favored with communications. In the *Odyssey* Odysseus himself is an interpreter of dreams (XIX., 535), and Helen explains omens from the flight of birds (XV., 172). Kalchas, indeed, seems to be the only case of an augur who is not heard of except for his augury. Helenos, who holds the corresponding position of soothsayer to the Trojans, is son

of Priam ; we do not hear that he is a priest, and he fights like any hero. But indeed it is true that the Homeric priests in no case form a caste apart, as they do in most civilized communities ; they generally fight with the rest."

89. **aton'd.** Observe the original meaning : at — one.

92. **Calchas the wise.** Observe this Grecian priest. He has no political power, and commands little reverence. In Agamemnon's treatment of him, as well as Chryses, is seen the relation of the religion to the government. It was neither master nor slave. — E. P. P. "The Mantis or soothsayer, whose skill was in most cases supposed to be hereditary, accompanied a Greek force on all its expeditions, and no prudent general would risk a battle or engage in any important enterprise without first ascertaining from this authority the will of the gods as shadowed out in certain appearances of the sacrifice or some peculiarity in the flight of the birds, or some phenomena of the heavens."

117. **blameless.** Pope, speaking of this adjective, says: "It is not only applied to a priest, but to one who, being conscious of the truth, prepares with an honest boldness to discover it."

124. **black-ey'd maid.** The Greek has been variously explained. The choice is thought to lie between "rolling the eyes" and "sparkling-eyed." It is not the color of the eye that is meant, but vivacity and youthful brightness.

143. **Clytæmnestra.** Wife of Agamemnon. Upon Agamemnon's return to Mycene he was murdered by her, and the murder was avenged by her son Orestes.

151-154. Agamemnon's demand for a fresh prize of honor

is not mere selfishness and avarice. It is clear throughout the *Iliad*, says Leaf, that it is in the public gifts, which are the signs of preëminence, that the point of honor lies ; to lose such a meed of honor is a disgrace as well as a material loss. So Achilles himself requires (XXIV., 175) that if he is to give up the body of Hector, he shall receive the ransom ; by so doing he does not diminish the grace of his act, but only saves himself from the reproach of weakness. It is important that this should be kept in view throughout the *Iliad*.

158–159. During the past years of the siege raids had been made upon the neighboring cities of the Troad.

177. **mighty Ajax.** The mightiest of the Grecian heroes, after Achilles, was the son of Telamon and cousin of Achilles. He was of vast stature and strength.

187. **Creta's king.** Idomeneus.

201. **Phthia.** The chief city of Thessaly, land of Achilles and his myrmidons.

228. **monarch's right.**
" There's such divinity doth hedge a king."
Kings are frequently called Zeus-nurtured.

231. The original is almost exactly equivalent to the line :
" Death and destruction dog thee at the heels,"
addressed by Queen Elizabeth to Dorset in *King Richard III.*

239. **Myrmidons.** The followers of Achilles.

265. **confess'd.** Revealed.

298. The abusive epithets with which this speech is charged are characteristic of the violence of Achilles and the plain speaking of Homer, which Pope too often tries to smooth and to make respectable.

309. sacred sceptre. One not belonging to Achilles, but which is handed by the herald to the speaker as a sign that he is in possession of the house. Tylor observes that in the Ellice Islands in the Pacific Ocean the natives "preserved an old worm-eaten staff, which in their assemblies the orator held in his hand as the sign of having the right to speak."

315. laws and justice. Literally precedents. The traditions are deposited as a sacred mystery in the keeping of the kings. In old Iceland and Ireland law was a tradition preserved entirely by the special knowledge of a few men.

326. golden studs. Nails which fastened the blade to the handle. (Leaf.)

331. Nestor. The orator of the Pylians. Pylos was in the Peloponnesus. He is represented as having lived through more than two generations and still being a king in the third; that is, between his seventieth and one hundredth years.

347-357. Pirithous. King of the Lapithæ, a mythical race of Thessaly, to which belonged **Dryas, Ceneus,** and **Polyphemus** (not the Cyclops). **Theseus,** king of Athens, gave friendly aid to Pirithous in the war which is referred to (line 357) between the Lapithæ and the Centaurs. The Centaurs of Homer are simply a savage people; there is no evidence that Homer conceived them the monsters of Greek fable.

355–357. Notice the substitution of the triplet for the distich.

371. **join'd.** Not an imperfect rhyme in Pope's time, nor in some places in our own. Whittier is true to the New England ear when he rhymes *line — join*.

412. The sea was regarded by the Greeks as a great ceremonial purifier. The meaning is that the Achaians washed in the sea so that it might carry off the defilements which were typical of their sin. Probably they had during the pestilence abstained from ablution, and cast dust on their heads in sign of mourning. It was no doubt by a survival from Greek times that the Neapolitans used, even down to 1580 A.D., to perform once a year a ritual ablution in the sea.   (Leaf.)

421. **Talthybius and Eurybates.** Legendary names of heralds generally. The former was the name of the hereditary heralds of Sparta, the latter that of the herald of Odysseus.

460. **parent goddess.** He cries, and his goddess-mother hears him —

> " Beside her aged father where she sat,
>   In the deep ocean-caves."

It is the original of our own Milton's beautiful invocation in " Comus " — the rough simple outline on which he has painted with a grace and fulness which make it all his own —

> " Sabrina fair !
>   Listen, where thou art sitting
>   Under the glassy, cool, translucent wave,
>   In twisted braids of lilies, knitting
>   The loose train of thy amber-dropping hair;

> Listen for dear honour's sake,
> Goddess of the silver lake,
> Listen, and save!"

Thetis hears, and rises on the sea — "like as it were a mist" — (the "White Lady of Avenel"), caresses him soothingly with her hand, as though the stalwart warrior were still a child indeed, and asks him the simple question which all mothers, goddesses or not, would put into much the same words, — "My son, why weepest thou?" (Collins.)

461. **severe a doom.** Achilles had been given the choice of a long inglorious life or a brief career full of honor. The doom is stated in Book IX. : —

> "My fates long since by Thetis were disclos'd,
> And each alternate, life or fame, propos'd;
> Here if I stay before the Trojan town,
> Short is my date, but deathless my renown:
> If I return, I quit immortal praise
> For years on years and long-extended days."

469. **aged Ocean.** In later mythology, Nereus, but the name does not occur in Homer, who has merely "her aged sire."

478. **Thebe.** A town in the Troad.

479. **Eëtion.** The father of Andromache, killed by Achilles.

515–529. "This strange legend of the binding of Zeus is not known from other sources, nor is it again mentioned in Homer, although there are numerous allusions to battles and quarrels among the gods, and to the previous dynasty of the Titans, who are now banished to Tartarus. It is particularly strange to find Athene in revolt against her father, in alliance with Hera, and the primitive earth-power Briareus on the side of Zeus. Nor do we find elsewhere in Homer any such monstrous conception as that of a being with a hundred arms." (Leaf.)

519. warlike maid. Minerva. **monarch of the main.** Neptune.

531. Embrace his knees. Suppliants threw themselves at the feet of the person to whom the supplication was addressed and embraced his knees, at the same time putting the right hand beneath his chin. See line 650. It has been suggested that the origin of the custom is in the action of the wounded warrior who with the left arm clasps the knee of his victor to hamper his movement, and with the right hand turns aside his face so that he cannot aim the fatal blow until he has heard the appeal for mercy.

555. warm limits. Oceanus, the great stream that flows round the world.

557. Æthiopia's blameless race. The Æthiopians dwelt on the extreme limits of the world, on the stream of Ocean. Whenever Homer alludes to the Æthiopians, it is always in terms of admiration and praise. They are famed for their piety, and the gods often make journeys to enjoy their feasts. George Eliot suggests that the Æthiopians were "blameless" because they lived so far off that they had no neighbors to criticise them.

576. dome. House, or temple. Latin : *Domus.*

586, 587, 600–613. A most exact account of the ancient sacrifices : first, the purification by the washing of hands ; second, the offering up of prayers ; third, the barley-cakes thrown upon the victim ; fourth, the manner of killing it, with the head turned upwards ; fifth, selecting the thighs and fat for their gods, as the best of the sacrifice, and disposing about them pieces cut from every part for a representation of the whole ; sixth, the libation of wine ; seventh, consuming the thighs in the fire of the altar ; eighth, the sacrificers dressing and feasting on the rest, with joy and hymns to the gods.

609. **instruments.** Five-tined flesh-hooks.

619. **Pæans.** Hymns to propitiate the god (originally sung in honor of Apollo) ; also a song of thanksgiving. It was sung by several persons.

630. "It was the custom to draw the ships entirely upon the shore, and to secure them by long props." (Felton.)

683–687. Literally rendered the passage reads : "The son of Kronos spoke, and bowed his dark brow, and the ambrosial locks waved from the king's immortal head ; and he made great Olympus shake." It is said (by Strabo) that this description inspired Phidias with the conception of his famous statue of Zeus at Olympia.

714. **Saturnius.** Son of Saturn (Kronos).

719. **consult.** How used and how accented ?

731. An intrusion of Pope's philosophy, not Homer's.

736. "The scene between Zeus and Hera is typical of the spirit in which Homer treats the deities of Olympia. It is, to say the least, not reverent, and far removed from any conception of primitive piety. It is, indeed, one among many signs that the civilization of the heroic age was old and not young —

a civilization which was outgrowing the simple faith of its ancestors. It has often been pointed out with truth that the humor of Homer is almost entirely confined to the scenes in Olympos, which seem to be treated as a fit opportunity for the display of passions which would be beneath the dignity of heroes. Even in morality the tone of Olympos is distinctly beneath that of earth. Mr. Gladstone has well remarked that not one of the gods can be called as distinctly *good* as the swineherd Eumaios.

741. **architect divine.** Fabled to be the fashioner of the Olympian palaces.

753. **double bowl.** Pope evidently has in mind the bowl with a cup at each end which was seen upon the table in Queen Anne's time. It is, however, a *two-handed* cup, such as has been found at Hissarlik and Mykenai.

760. Refers to an old fable of Jupiter's hanging up Juno and flogging her.

760–765.

> " Nor was his name unheard or unadored
> In ancient Greece ; and in Ausonian land
> Men called him Mulciber ; and how he fell
> From heaven they fabled, thrown by angry Jove
> Sheer o'er the crystal battlements ; from morn
> To noon he fell, from noon to dewy eve,
> A summer's day ; and with the setting sun
> Dropped from the zenith, like a falling star,
> On Lemnos, the Ægean isle." — *Paradise Lost*, I., 738.

765. **Sinthians.** The inhabitants of Lemnos, an island sacred to Hephaistos because of the volcano Mosychlos. Their name is derived from their piratical habits.

771. The lame Vulcan, assuming the office of Hebe or Gany-
mede, stops the heavenly quarrel by making himself the subject
of merriment.

BOOK VI

Of all the *Iliad* this incomparable book attains the grandest
heights of narrative and composition, of action and pathos.
Nowhere else have we so perfect a gallery of types of human
character ; the two pairs, Hector and Paris, Helen and Andromache, in their truthfulness and contrast, form a group as subtly
as they are broadly drawn ; while, on the other hand, the
"battle vignettes" with which the book opens, and the culmination of the scenes of war in the meeting of Glaukos and
Diomedes, set before us with unequalled vivacity the pride of
life of an heroic age, the refinement of feeling which no fierce-
ness of fight can barbarize, in the most consummate manner of
the "great style." (Leaf.)

5. **fam'd streams.** Homer names the Simois and Xanthus
(which men call Scamandar). The Simois rose in Mount Ida,
and the Xanthus near Troy ; they formed a junction before
they reached the Hellespont.

7. **Ajax.** The son of Telamon is always meant by Homer
when no epithet is used to distinguish him from the other Ajax,
who was the son of Oileus. Ajax commences his exploits on
the departure of the gods from the battle. It is observed of this
hero that he is never assisted by the gods.

9. Notice the grammatical construction : *Falcion* is the subject of *found* and *hewed*.

16. **Axylus** was distinguished for his hospitality. This trait was characteristic of the Oriental nations, and is often alluded to by the ancient writers. The right of hospitality often united families belonging to different and hostile nations, and was even transmitted from father to son. This description is a fine tribute to the generosity of Axylus. (Felton.)

24. **His faithful servant.** Calesius was the driver of Axylus's chariot.

28. **Naiad.** The fountain-nymph Abarbarea.

36. **hell.** The underworld.

37. **Teucer.** Son of Telemon and step-brother of Ajax, renowned for his archery.

38. **Nestor's son.** Antilochus.

41. **Pedasus.** A town of Mysia.

46. **Spartan spear.** In the hands of Menelaus.

49. **tamarisk.** Not a large tree, as Pope imagines. In the original the horses stumble in a tamarisk's bough and so snap short the pole of the chariot.

61–62. **told.** Counted; *tellan*, to count. Coined money was not in use at this time. The gifts for ransom are bronze and "smithied iron."

80. Pope commenting upon the fact that Agamemnon's cruelty is not blamed by Homer ascribes it to the uncivilized manners of those times. Homer very rarely expresses any moral judgment upon the action of his characters. The historical books of the Old Testament abound in similar cruelties to conquered enemies.

88. This maxim of war, "To the victor belong the spoils," is very naturally introduced. According to Dacier it was for such lessons as these that Alexander so much esteemed Homer.

91. **Helenus.** Son of Priam.

108. **our mother.** Hecuba.

113. **mantle.** Helenus directs Hector to enter the city and cause the Trojan women to assemble in the temple of Minerva with a robe or *peplos* for a propitiatory offering, and to promise a sacrifice if Athene will stay the victorious progress of Agamemnon. In one of the scenes portrayed in the frieze of the Parthenon a *peplos* is solemnly brought to the goddess by the city of Athens.

145. Hector's shield reaches from the ankles to the neck. It was composed of layers of ox-hide covered with metal. The hides were turned up at the outer edge of the shield to form a rim and so prevent any friction against the edge of the metal facing. Hector walks with his shield hanging at his back.

148. "The episode of Glaucus and Diomedes is remarkable in several respects. At first sight it seems improbable that two combatants, eager to engage, should hold a dialogue of this description ; and accordingly we find a writer in the *Edinburgh Review* objecting to and ridiculing it as in the highest degree absurd. It must be remembered that Homer is describing the manners of an ancient heroic age and not the nineteenth century. His battles are not like those of Waterloo and Austerlitz, the result of scientific calculation, and dependent on the movements of masses of men, giving but little scope to individual prowess and, above all, are not decided by powder and bullet.

They are the battles of an age of simplicity, in which the personal valour of the chieftains bore a distinguished share. It happened not infrequently that opposing chieftains singled each other out and fought hand to hand, after holding parley and making various interrogations of each other. This has indeed occurred in the skirmishing warfare of the last Greek Revolution. We have before adverted to the right of hospitality. It cannot be deemed improbable that two warriors, whose fathers had exchanged courtesies and pledges of this description, should meet on the field of battle and upon inquiry find themselves thus bound together. The peculiar sacredness of this tie would cause them at once to suspend hostilities and perhaps exchange tokens of friendly recognition. On the whole this episode, so far from being an unnatural and improbable excrescence, is a relief to the carnage and confusion of the battle and presents a beautiful picture of that feature of ancient society which has already been the subject of remark." (Felton.)

150. **mark'd for war,** *i.e.* for single combat, as in "Sohrab and Rustum."

161. The home of Lycurgus was in Thrace; "Nyssa's sacred grove" is not geographical. He drove Bacchus, Dionysos, and his followers (Bacchantes) from his domains and was punished by Zeus with blindness. The "consecrated spears" (line 165) should be "wands" or staves wreathed with ivy, which were carried by the Mænads, or Bacchantes.

191. **Æolian.** Son of Æolus.

193. **Ephyre.** The early name of Corinth.

201. **Antea.** The wife of Prœtus.

L

208. " Prœtus, unwilling himself to violate the laws of hospitality by killing a guest, sends him to Antea's father, Iobates, who likewise after entertaining Bellerophon shrinks from slaying him and sends him into perils which he expects to prove fatal."

210. This passage raises the important question of the knowledge of writing in Homeric times. It seems impossible to deny that such a knowledge is implied. The "folded tablet" seems to show that the message might have been intelligible to Bellerophon if it had not been concealed ; the "many deadly" (literally *soul-destroying*) "things" implies a real message, not a mere picture or conventional sign of a murder or the like. It is further clear that the use of such a letter of introduction was regular, for the king asks to see it as a matter of course. This is, in fact, just an example of the way in which we might suppose writing to have been introduced into Greece. It seems to be regarded as a strange accomplishment, for the adjective "soul-destroying" implies a sort of magical power, such as always is ascribed to writing by savages who are not practically acquainted with it. It is known only to a royal family connected with Asia Minor, and it is to Asia Minor that we are being more and more led by recent researches to look for the introduction of the higher culture into Greece. There is therefore no reason for doubting that the knowledge of the art had gone so far as this passage indicates long before the Dorian invasion. This, of course, is far from justifying us in supposing that an Achaian poet would be able to use writing for the composition of a long poem, though it does show that this is not

impossible. If we ask what sort of writing this could have been, we naturally think of the Cypriote syllabary. It is hardly likely that the Phœnician alphabet, the foundation of later Greek writing, had been yet introduced, for the traces of Phœnician influence on the Achaian world are very few and slight, just as the mention of the Phœnicians in the *Iliad* is rare. The Cypriote syllabary, on the other hand, must have been known at an early date throughout Asia Minor, if Professor Sayce is right in recognizing it on whorls from Hissarlik. We may thus provisionally suppose it to be alluded to here in the hope of further discoveries to elucidate this all-important point. The other alternative is that the writing may have been Egyptian, for it is daily becoming more clear that the Achaians had been acquainted with Egypt from a date long anterior to the Homeric poems, and it is likely enough that they may have picked up some knowledge of the use of hieroglyphs. In fact, a few Egyptian inscriptions are the only traces of writing which have as yet been found in Mykenai.

215. According to the ancient custom of hospitality the guest was entertained before he was questioned as to his name and message. Alkinoos entertained Odysseus a whole day before asking him his name.

219. **Chimæra.** The only instance in Homer of the fabulous mixed monsters of later Greek mythology.

226. **prodigies.** Portents.

227. **Solymæan crew.** The primitive inhabitants of Lykia, who were driven by the Lycians (from Crete) into the mountains.

229. **Amazons.** A race of warrior women.

242. Homer names them: Isandros, Hippolochos, and Laodameia.

247. **Aleian field.** The "Plain of Wandering" was believed to be in Cilicia. The tradition evidently was that Bellerophon became mad.

250. **Phœbe's dart.** Sudden death. *Women* died painlessly when smitten by *Phœbe* (Diana).

251. He died in battle.

274. **Tyrian dye.** Royal purple.

277–278. Refers to the expedition of the "Seven against Thebes."

290. Leaf remarks: "This curious ending to a delightful episode seems almost like a burlesque, and is hard to understand. Elsewhere in Homer the only characters treated with distinctly humorous intention are the gods." Pope mistranslates in line 291 when Homer says that "Zeus took from Glaukos his wits."

297. **Scæan gate.** The great gate of the city through which the Trojans went forth to battle.

298. **beech-tree.** *Oak-tree* in Homer.

314. **Laodice.** Daughter of Hecuba.

318. "There is a mournfulness in the interview between the hero and his mother which is deeply interesting. Her urging him to take wine and his refusal were natural and simple incidents which heighten the effect of the scene." (Felton.)

329–333. This homily upon temperance belongs to Pope not to Homer. The original has "bring me no honey-hearted wine, my mother, lest thou cripple me of my courage, and I be forgetful of my might."

362-363. **Tyre** and **Sidon** were famous for works in gold, embroidery, etc., and for whatever pertained to magnificence and luxury.

371. **Palladian dome.** *Dome* (or temple) of Pallas (Minerva).

372. **Theano.** Sister of Hecuba, and daughter of Cisseus, a prince of Thrace.

395. **ten cubits.** Sixteen feet (*eleven* cubits, as in Homer) was not an unusual length for a spear. Xenophon speaks of one fifteen cubits, or twenty-two feet.

396. **ringlets.** Meant to hold the head of the spear in place and prevent the wood from splitting.

399-401. "The employment in which Hector finds Paris engaged is extremely characteristic." (Felton.) Paris carries his foppish airs into the affairs of war.

403. **instructs their hands.** Working at the loom.

466. **second joy.** That is, after her husband.

467. **Astyanax.** The only son of Hector. The name means "defender of the city," as Hector means "protector." See lines 501-503.

491. Here we are introduced to the second female character in the poem. It is as the wife and mother that Andromache charms us. It has been remarked that Homer never applies to her any epithet implying personal attractions, though all his translators, Lord Derby included, have been tempted to do so.

Hector meets her at the Scæan gate with the nurse and the child. The father looks silently on his boy and smiles; Andromache in tears clings to her husband and makes a pathetic appeal to him not to be too prodigal of a life which is so dear to his wife and child. He is now "her father, mother, brother, husband," — her all. "The incidents which follow are simple but requisite. Hector wishes to take in his arms his beloved son; but the child, terrified by the glittering armor and the waving crest, clings to the bosom of the nurse. This calls a smile upon the countenance of the parents, who are thus, by a happy stroke of nature, made to forget, for a single moment, the gloomy state of public affairs in affection for their offspring. Hector lays upon the ground his shining helmet, caresses his son, and utters a prayer becoming a patriot and warrior. He places the child in the arms of his wife, who receives him upon her 'fragrant bosom,' smiling tearfully. This is one of the most beautiful expressions to be found in any language. It is concise yet distinct, and presents a perfect image of mingled gentleness and sadness. It fills the imagination and touches the heart." (Felton.)

528–530. Pope amplifies Homer, who has "burnt him in his inlaid armour and raised a barrow over him; and all about were elm-trees planted by the mountain nymphs, daughters of ægis-bearing Zeus." It was a universal custom among the primitive Aryan nations to bury a warrior's arms with his dead body. Swords have been found in graves at Mykenai.

539. **Hippoplacia.** More correctly Hyppoplacia, another name for Phœbe.

583. **Hyperia's spring.** Homer says "from fount Messeis or Hyperia." The former is in Laconia, the latter in Thessaly. "The mention of these with Argos may perhaps indicate Menelaos of Sparta, Achilles of Thessaly, and Agamemnon of Argos as the three probable masters of Andromache." (Döderlein.) Later tradition has it that Andromache became the prize of Neoptolemus, son of Achilles.

676–679. Hector resumes his hope of success and his spirit is roused again as he approaches the field of battle. The close of the book in Homer is much stronger than in Pope's poor paraphrase. "All this will we make good hereafter, if Zeus ever vouchsafe us to set before the heavenly gods, that are for everlasting, the cup of deliverance in our halls, when we have chased out of Troyland the well-greaved Achaians."

BOOK XXII

The preceding book closed with Achilles in pursuit of Apollo, who had assumed the disguise of the Trojan Agenor in order to draw Achilles away from the field of battle, that the Trojans might have an opportunity to retreat into the city.

6. **roof of shields.** The Greeks held their shields above their heads for protection against missiles thrown from the walls.

30. Homer makes Achilles say to Apollo in wrath: "Verily, I would avenge me on thee had I but the power."

39. **Orion's dog.** Sirius in the constellation *canis major*, so called from its proximity to the constellation Orion. When Sirius rose with the sun in summer it was supposed to exert an

evil influence, to cause fevers, etc. Hence this time of year was called the *canicular* or dog days. **Weighs** means presses to its close.

43. " With how much dreadful Pomp is Achilles here introduced ? How noble, and in what bold colours hath he drawn the blazing of his Arms, the Rapidity of his Advance, the Terror of his Appearance, the Desolation around him, but above all the certain Death attending all his motions and his very looks ; what a crowd of terrible Ideas in this one Simile ! But immediately after this follows the moving Image of the two aged Parents, trembling, weeping, and imploring their Son ! This is succeeded again by the dreadful, gloomy picture of Hector, all on fire, obstinate, bent on Death, and expecting Achilles, admirably painted in the Simile of the Snake rolled up in his Den and collecting his Poisons. And indeed thro' the whole Book the wonderful Contrast and Opposition of the Moving and of the Terrible is perpetually kept each heightening the other. I can't find words to express how so great Beauties affect me." (Pope.)

45. **obtests.** Entreats.

64. **mother.** Homer names her Laothoë. She is the daughter of Altes and a wife of Priam. This passage is quoted as a genuine case of polygamy, but among the Trojans only ; nothing of the sort is even hinted at among the Homeric Greeks. The deaths of Polydore and Lycaon are described at the end of Book XX. and the beginning of XXI.

69. **Lelegia's throne.** The Leleges were supposed to live on the coast of Asia Minor and the islands of the Ægean.

71. **Stygian coast.** The underworld, inhabited by the spirits of the dead.

112. **The zone unbrac'd.** Hecuba unfastened the brooch by which her robe was fastened over the right shoulder. This would allow the upper fold of the front of the robe to fall so that the breast would be shown.

132. The poison of snakes was supposed to be derived from herbs which they ate when about to attack.

137. This speech of Hector shows the fluctuation of his mind, with much discernment on the part of the poet. He breaks out, after having apparently meditated a return to the city. But the imagined reproaches of Polydamas, and the anticipated scorn of the Trojans, forbid it. He soliloquizes upon the possibility of coming to terms with Achilles, and offering him large concessions; but the character of Achilles precludes all hope of reconciliation. It is a fearful crisis with him, and his mind wavers, as if presentiment of his approaching doom. (Felton.)

140. When the Greeks were fighting for the corpse of Patroclus, Achilles appeared and, shouting, frightened the Trojans. Polydamas advised to retire within the city for the night, but Hector favored camping on the field, and his command was obeyed.

157. **terms of peace.** They are stated in lines 158–163.

158. Helen and the treasure that was carried away with her.

175. **The Pelian jav'lin.** Patroclus when putting on the armor of Achilles "seized two strong lances that fitted his

grasp, only he took not the spear of the noble son of Æacus, heavy and huge and stalwart, that none other of the Achaians could wield, but Achilles alone availed to wield it : even the ashen Pelian spear that Chiron gave to his father dear, from a peak of Pelian, to be the death of warriors."

180. Hector's sudden flight at the approach of Achilles is one of the most extraordinary incidents of the *Iliad*. Says Mr. Andrew Lang: "In a saga or a *chanson de geste*, in an Arthurian romance, in a Border ballad, in whatever poem or tale answers in our Northern literature, however feebly, to Homer, this flight round the walls of Troy would be an absolute impossibility. Under the eyes of his father, his mother, his countrymen, Hector flies — the gallant Hector, 'a very perfect, gentle knight' — from the onset of a single foe." But, Mr. Lang adds: "Homer's world, Homer's chivalry, Homer's ideas of knightly honor, were all unlike those of the Christian and the Northern world."

Professor Mahaffy, on the other hand, regards this slur and other slurs on Hector's courage as changes wrought by alien hands in the original poem. "Why," he asks, "is he so important all through the plot of the poem? Why is his death by Achilles made an achievement of the highest order? Why are the chiefs who at one time challenge and worst him, at another quaking with fear at his approach? Simply because in the original plan of the *Iliad* he *was* a great warrior, and because these perpetual defeats by Diomede and Ajax, this avoidance of Agamemnon, this swaggering and 'hectoring,' which we now find in him, were introduced by the enlargers and interpolators

in order to enhance the merits of their favorites at his expense."
(Maxwell and Chubb.)

189. **fore-right.** Right to the fore, straight ahead.

193. **fig-trees.** They have been mentioned in Book VI. as a
landmark. The wagon road runs round the wall at a short distance from it. **Smoke.** Raise a dust by their speed.

201. **marble cisterns.** Contrast this with Homer's "broad
beautiful washing-troughs of stone."

241. **Tritonia.** Trito-born, an epithet of Athene (Minerva).

"Tritonia's airy shrine adorns
Colonna's cliff, and gleams along the wave." — BYRON.

247. **vapour.** Scent.

251. **Dardan.** Dardan is frequently equivalent to Trojan or
Ilian. The Dardanians (usually of wider designation than
Trojan) were led by Æneas.

257. "The inability to catch and escape is vividly compared
to the feeling of being bound to pursue, and yet of being rooted
to the ground, which is so common in nightmare." Cowper
remarks that "the numbers in the original are so constructed
as to express the painful struggle that characterizes such a
dream."

276. **hell receives the weight.** Hector is doomed to Hades.

291. **Deïphobus.** Minerva assumes the form of Hector's
brother, son of Priam and Hecuba.

293. **show.** Appearance.

294. Mr. Lang says: "It is remarkable that when the true

poet had to pit against each other a courteous and patriotic
warrior like Hector and a young hero who, like Achilles, is
really fighting only for his own hand and his private passion, he
should have made Hector check our sympathy by his flight, and
Achilles even more unsympathetic by the treacherous aid of
Athene than by his own relentless and savage revenge." To a
Greek audience, Mr. Leaf thinks: "The presence of the gods on
Achilles' side was not so much a mere extraneous aid as a tan-
gible sign that Achilles was, after all, fighting the great fight of
Hellenism against barbarism; it is a reminder that the action
on earth is but a reflexion of the will of heaven, and exalts
rather than belittles those to whom the help is given." "It is
a cardinal rule with Homer," says Mr. Gladstone, "that no
considerable Greek chieftain is ever slain in fair fight by a
Trojan."

348. In Book XVIII., Thetis, Achilles's mother, had told him
that straightway after Hector's death was death appointed unto
him. In Book XIX., his horse Xanthus, gifted for the moment
with human speech and the power of prophecy, had foretold
that his master's death-day was nigh at hand. Mr. John Add-
ington Symonds thinks that the knowledge of his own approaching end is the key to the terrible ferocity displayed by the Greek
chieftain. "Stung as he is," says Mr. Symonds, "by remorse
and by the sorrow for Patroclus, which does not unnerve him,
but rather kindles his whole spirit to a flame, we are prepared
to see him fierce even to cruelty. But when we know that in
the midst of the carnage he is himself moving a dying man,
when we remember that he is sending his slain foes like mes-

sengers before his face to Hades, when we keep the warning words of Thetis and Xanthus in our minds, then the grim frenzy of Achilles becomes dignified. The world is in a manner over for him, and he appears the incarnation of disdainful anger and revengeful love, the conscious scourge of God and instrument of destiny."

391. **Jove's bird.** The eagle.

395. **fourfold cone.** Four-plated helmet.

397. **Vulcanian frame.** Forged by Vulcan.

405-406. Achilles says, lamenting the death of Patroclus (Book XVIII.): "Hector that slew him hath stripped from him the armour great and fair, a wonder to behold, that the gods gave to Peleus."

436. **prevalence.** Efficacy.

437. Mr. Leaf interprets the line: "As surely as I cannot eat thee myself so surely the dogs shall eat thee."

452. The prophecy is fulfilled when Achilles is killed by a poisoned arrow shot by Paris and guided by Apollo.

466. The admiration expressed for the beauty of the corpse is thoroughly Greek.

467. The mutilation of the body is palliated by the widespread belief that the spirit is deprived of the power to revenge when the body is mutilated.

494. The full text of this song of triumph is: "Great glory have we won; we have slain the noble Hector, unto whom the Trojans prayed throughout their city, as he had been a god."

610. This notion of astrology is, of course, Pope's, not Homer's.

640. The idea seems to be that an orphan is deprived of the favor of the gods and may be insulted with impunity. This idea still lives in Albania, where at the marriage ceremony the marriage loaf must be baked by a maid whose parents are alive or she will bring misfortune to the wedded pair.

BOOK XXIV

"The supreme beauty of the last book of the *Iliad*, and the divine pathos of the dying fall, in which the tale of strife and blood passes away, are above all words of praise. The meeting of Priam and Achilles, the kissing of the deadly hands, and the simplicity of infinite sadness over man's fate in Achilles' reply, mark the high tide of a great epoch of poetry. In them we feel that the whole range of suffering has been added to the unsurpassed presentment of action which, without this book, might seem to be the crowning glory of the *Iliad*." (Leaf.)

1. **games.** The funeral games in honor of Patroclus were described in Book XXIII.

20. Achilles wanders aimlessly.

25. **monument.** A funeral mound. The bones of Patroclus were placed in the tent of Achilles.

33. **golden shield.** Literally, golden ægis: a perplexing passage, for the ægis belongs to Zeus, not to Apollo.

34. **Hermes.** This is the first allusion to Mercury as a thieving god.

37. Empress Juno (Hera).

38-41. This is the sole occasion in the *Iliad* where any allusion is made to the story of the contest of beauty and the judgment of Paris, which led to the flight of Helen.

41. Cyprian queen. So called from the island where Venus was first worshipped.

56-57. Cowper explains that shame is a man's blessing if he is properly influenced by it, or his curse in its consequences if he is deaf to its dictates. Mr. Leaf says that the Greek word translated *shame* expresses on the one hand the respect for the opinion of men which we call sense of honor; on the other, it can stand for the wrong shame or want of proper boldness, such as prevents a man from properly doing his work in the world.

96. azure queen. Thetis.

99. Iris. Goddess of the rainbow; the messenger of Jupiter, as Mercury is of all Olympus.

103. Samos. Should be Samothrace.

108. This remarkable simile is badly translated. The original reads: "And she sped to the bottom like a weight of lead that, mounted on horn of a field-ox, goeth down, bearing death to the ravenous fishes." It would appear that a little tube or horn was passed over the line just above the hook, to prevent the fish biting it through, and some molten lead was run into the tube to sink it.

112. blue-hair'd sisters. The Nereids.

146. **glory.** The glory accorded to Achilles is the receipt of gifts wherein the heroic point of honor lies.

285. **chargers.** Large dishes.

289–290. Homer says more clearly: "Yet not that even did the old man grudge from his halls, for he was exceeding fain at heart to ransom his dear son."

311. **erring.** Errare, to wander.

322. This is the only time when Troilus, a favorite character in the later tale of Troy, is mentioned in the *Iliad*.

336. **ringlets.** Through which the reins were passed.

346. The car conveying the presents was drawn by mules; the other, in which Priam and the herald rode, was drawn by horses. The Mysians of northern Asia Minor were famous for breeding mules.

359. Zeus.

361. The eagle.

375. **the mid pavement.** That is, in the midst of the court, because the altar of Zeus is there.

390. **Percnos.** The black eagle.

393. **dexter.** Appearing on the right.

418. **incumbent.** Resting upon.

430. **silver spring.** Homer says: "At the river," that is, Scamander.

431. **Ilus' ancient marble.** The barrow or tomb of Ilus, grandfather of Priam.

457. **lines.**   Lineaments, features.

552. **Pelides' lofty tent.**   The tent of Achilles is described as though it were a palace.   It has a hall with fore court, vestibule, and colonnades, and is at times spoken of as a house. This indicates a complete difference of view from the rest of the *Iliad*.

572. **his son.**   Neoptolemus ; Alexander the Great claimed descent from Achilles through this son.

586.   Of these lines Pope writes : "I fancy this Interview between Priam and Achilles would furnish an admirable subject for a Painter, in the Surprize of Achilles and the other spectators, the attitude of Priam and the sorrow in the countenance of this unfortunate king.   That circumstance of Priam kissing the Hands of Achilles is inimitably fine ; 'he kissed,' says Homer, 'the Hands of Achilles, those terrible, murderous Hands that had robbed him of so many Sons.'   By these two words the Poet recalls to our mind all the noble Actions performed by Achilles in the whole *Ilias;* and at the same time strikes us with the utmost Compassion for this unhappy king who is reduced so low as to be obliged to kiss those Hands that had slain his subjects and ruined his kingdom and family." — POPE'S *Homer*, 1st edition, 6, 211.

598–633.   "The whole scene between Achilles and Priam, when the latter comes to the Greek camp for the purpose of redeeming the body of Hector, is at once the most profoundly skilful, and yet the simplest and most affecting passage in the *Iliad*. . . .   Observe the exquisite taste of Priam in occupying the mind of Achilles, from the outset, with the image of his

M

father; in gradually introducing the parallel of his own situation ; and, lastly, mentioning Hector's name when he perceives that the hero is softened, and then only in such a manner as to flatter the pride of the conqueror. . . . The whole passage defies translation, for there is that about the Greek which has no name, but which is of so fine and ethereal a subtlety that it can only be felt in the original, and is lost in an attempt to transfuse it into another language." — H. N. COLERIDGE.

745. manes. Belongs to Roman mythology and means the spirits of the dead regarded as divinities of the household. Here it is the spirit of Patroclus.

757-759. As Niobe ate in her extreme grief, and she is the pattern of faithful sorrow, you may well eat without appearing hard of heart.

762. Cynthia. Diana, so called from Mount Cynthus, in the island of Delos, where she was born.

769. inhume. Bury.

773. herself a rock. Pausanias says of the figure of Niobe on Mount Cipylas near Smyrna : " The rock, seen from near at hand, is a precipice, with no resemblance to a woman, mourning or otherwise ; but if you go farther off you can fancy you are looking at a woman, downcast, and bathed in tears." Visitors to Smyrna are still shown this figure rudely carved by human hands.

775. Acheloüs. A river of Lydia.

776. wat'ry fairies. Fairies and their rings belong to modern tradition. It is the water nymphs of whom Homer speaks.

862. **Xanthus**. Scamander.

870. **Cassandra**. Daughter of Priam, and gifted with prophetic powers.

900. **melancholy choir**. The professional mourners.

906. "The affection of Hector for his wife, no less distinguished than the passion of Achilles for his friend, has made
the Trojan prince rather than his Greek rival the hero of
modern romance." (A. J. Symonds.)

934-935. These two lines are quoted from Congreve, to
whom Pope dedicated this translation.

962. "Helen is throughout the *Iliad* a genuine lady, graceful in motion and speech, noble in her associations, full of
remorse for a fault for which higher powers seem responsible,
yet grateful and affectionate towards those with whom that
fault had connected her. I have always thought the following
speech, in which Helen laments Hector and hints at her own
invidious and unprotected situation in Troy, as almost the
sweetest passage in the poem." (Henry Nelson Coleridge.)

1015-1016. Literally translated the last line of the *Iliad*
reads: "Thus held they funeral for Hector, tamer of horses,"
an ending worthy in its majestic simplicity of the praise with
which Cowper takes leave of a task to which he had been in-
debted for the smooth and easy flight of many thousand hours.
"I cannot take my leave of this noble poem," he says, "without expressing how much I am struck with this plain conclusion
of it. It is like the exit of a great man out of company whom
he has entertained magnificently; neither pompous nor familiar;

not contemptuous, yet without much ceremony. I recollect nothing, among the works of mere man, that exemplifies so strongly the true style of great antiquity."

THE TIME OF THE ACTION

I., 71.   The action of the *Iliad* occupies altogether fifty-one days, the distribution of which will show the argument of the poem.   The plague rages nine days; in the tents take place the quarrel between Agamemnon and Achilles, and the appeal of the latter to his mother, Thetis.   The return of Zeus is expected on the twelfth day from that date; on the twenty-first day, therefore, he gives the promise to honor Achilles by the defeat of the Greeks, upon which the further action of the poem hinges.   On the morning of the twenty-second, after the agitation caused by the dream of Agamemnon, commences the *first* battle, which, with the single combat between Paris and Menelaus, and that between Hector and Ajax, carries on the poem as far as Book VII., 440.   On the next morning a truce is made, and the burial of the dead and the construction, on the Greek side, of a fortification in front of their camp, occupy that and the following day.   On the twenty-fifth, therefore, Zeus holds the council in which he prohibits divine help from the war altogether, and the *second* battle is begun and ended at night with the defeat of the Greeks.   The night is then taken up by an embassy to Achilles and by a raid on the Trojan camp, in both of which measures Odysseus bears a principal part.   The twenty-sixth is the day of the *third* battle, which commences evenly, but is continued by the storming of the Greek rampart

(Book XII.), the attack on the fleet (Books XIII.-XV.), its rescue by Patroclus (Book XVI.), the struggle over that hero's body (Book XVII.), and the final retreat of Troy before the unarmed Achilles (Book XVIII.). On the twenty-seventh day Achilles receives his armor and is reconciled to Agamemnon, and before the evening has completed his revenge with the death of Hector in the *fourth* battle of the poem. The next two days are occupied in the preparation of the pyre of Patroclus, in the burning of his body, and in the games held in his honor. For eleven days more Achilles continues his insults to the body of Hector, so that it is not till the evening of the fortieth day that Priam comes to the camp for its recovery. On the morning of the forty-first he returns with the corpse and with the promise of a twelve days' truce. Nine days are then occupied in laments and preparations. On the tenth the pyre of Hector is built and burned, and on the eleventh, or fifty-first of the whole action, his bones are interred and the mound above them heaped. The night of that day is spent in the funeral feast, and the war is expected to recommence on the next morning. — J. G. CORDERY.

INDEX TO NOTES

BOOKS PRESCRIBED FOR COLLEGE ENTRANCE EXAMINATIONS.

For Reading.   1899.   *For Study.*

For Reading.

Cooper — Last of the Mohicans.
Dryden — Palamon and Arcite.
Addison — Sir Roger de Coverley.
Goldsmith — Vicar of Wakefield.
Coleridge — Ancient Mariner.
De Quincey — Revolt of the Tartars.
Pope — Iliad, Books I., VI., XXII., XXIV.

For Study.

Shakespeare — Macbeth.
Milton — Paradise Lost, Books I. and II.
Burke — Speech on Conciliation.
Carlyle — Essay on Burns.

For Reading.   1900.   *For Study.*

For Reading.

Tennyson — The Princess. ⌣
Scott — Ivanhoe. ✔
De Quincey — Revolt of the Tartars.
Pope — Iliad, Books I., VI., XXII., XXIV.
Cooper — Last of the Mohicans. ✔
Dryden — Palamon and Arcite.
Addison — Sir Roger de Coverley.
Goldsmith — Vicar of Wakefield. ✔

For Study.

Macaulay — Essays on Milton and Addison.
Burke — Speech on Conciliation.
Shakespeare — Macbeth.
Milton — Paradise Lost, Books I. and II.

THE MACMILLAN COMPANY,
66 FIFTH AVENUE, NEW YORK.

BOOKS PRESCRIBED FOR COLLEGE ENTRANCE EXAMINATIONS.

For Reading. **1901.** *For Study.*

Eliot — Silas Marner.
Shakespeare — Macbeth.
Pope — Iliad, Books I., VI., XXII., XXIV.
Addison — Sir Roger de Coverley.
Goldsmith — Vicar of Wakefield.
Coleridge — Ancient Mariner.
Tennyson — The Princess.
Scott — Ivanhoe.
Cooper — Last of the Mohicans.

Shakespeare — Macbeth.
Milton — L'Allegro, Il Penseroso, Comus, and Lycidas.
Burke — Speech on Conciliation.
Macaulay — Essays on Milton and Addison.

For Reading. **1902.** *For Study.*

Pope — Iliad, Books I., VI., XXII., XXIV.
Addison — Sir Roger de Coverley.
Coleridge — Ancient Mariner.
Eliot — Silas Marner.
Shakespeare — Merchant of Venice.
Tennyson — The Princess.
Scott — Ivanhoe.
Cooper — Last of the Mohicans.
Goldsmith — Vicar of Wakefield.

Shakespeare — Macbeth.
Burke — Speech on Conciliation.
Milton — L'Allegro, Il Penseroso, Comus, and Lycidas.
Macaulay — Essays on Milton and Addison.

THE MACMILLAN COMPANY,
66 FIFTH AVENUE, NEW YORK.

Exercises in Rhetoric and English Composition.

By GEORGE R. CARPENTER,

Professor of Rhetoric and English Composition, Columbia College.

HIGH SCHOOL COURSE.   SEVENTH EDITION.

16mo.   Cloth.   Price 75 cents, *net.*

ADVANCED COURSE.   FOURTH EDITION.

12mo.   Cloth.   Price $1.00, *net.*

" This work gives the student the very gist and germ of the art of composition." — *Public Opinion.*

" G. R. Carpenter, Professor of Rhetoric and English Composition in Columbia College, has prepared a work under the title of ' Exercises in Rhetoric and English Composition,' in which not so much the science of Rhetoric is mapped out and defined as the practical workings of the art are furnished to the student with just enough of the principles to guide him aright.   The author gives an abundance of exercises for the student to study and analyze, and this is the very best kind of help.   The scheme of the subject-matter is somewhat unique and novel, but it is comprehensive and lucid. . . .   A very serviceable and suggestive book to read and consult." — *Education.*

" The text represents the substance of teaching which a freshman may fairly be expected to compass, and it is set forth with a clearness and directness and brevity so admirable as to make the volume seem almost the realization of that impossible short method of learning to write which has often been sought for, but never with a nearer approach to being found. . . .   We do not hesitate to give unreserved commendation to this little book." — *The Nation.*

" Seldom has so much good common sense been put within so brief a space." — *The Boston Herald.*

THE MACMILLAN COMPANY,

66 FIFTH AVENUE, NEW YORK.

Studies in Structure and Style.

BASED ON SEVEN MODERN ENGLISH ESSAYS.

By W. T. BREWSTER, A.M.,
Tutor in Rhetoric and English in Columbia University.

With an Introduction by G. R. CARPENTER, A.B., Professor of Rhetoric and English Composition in Columbia University.

Cloth. 12mo. $1.10.

The Seven Essays referred to are : J. A. Froude's "The Defeat of the Spanish Armada," R. L. Stevenson's "Personal Experience and Review," John Morley's "Macaulay," Matthew Arnold's "On the Study of Celtic Literature," James Bryce's "The Strength of American Democracy," John Ruskin's "The Crown of Wild Olive," and J. H. Newman's "What is a University?"

It is of too recent publication to have been in class-room use, but will be introduced at the beginning of another school year in a number of schools.

"It is well conceived, and the selections are excellent for their purpose." — **Prof. Felix E. Schelling,** *University of Pennsylvania.*

"The selections seem to be chosen with good judgment, and the notes to be careful and instructive." — **Prof. Fred P. Emery,** *Dartmouth College, Hanover, N.H.*

"I am even more pleased with the book than I had expected to be. . . . I shall certainly try to introduce the book into one of my classes next fall." — **Miss Anna H. Smith,** *High School, Binghamton, N.Y.*

"'Studies in Structure and Style' is, I think, the best book of the kind that has yet appeared, and I shall be glad to recommend it to my classes." — **Prof. Edwin M. Hopkins,** *University of Kansas, Lawrence, Kan.*

"I have delayed to acknowledge Brewster's 'Studies in Structure and Style,' which you kindly sent me, until I could examine it with some care. That examination is very satisfactory. The selections are well chosen, and the comments both on their structure and their style are distinctly valuable. The work can hardly fail to be of large service." — **Miss E. G. Willcox,** *Wellesley College, Mass.*

THE MACMILLAN COMPANY,

66 FIFTH AVENUE, NEW YORK.

www.ingramcontent.com/pod-product-compliance
Lightning Source LLC
Chambersburg PA
CBHW022001050726
47498CB00007BA/2348